The Memoir
of the Minotaur

The Memoir
of the Minotaur

Tom Shachtman

Lake Dallas, Texas

FIRST EDITION

The Memoir of the Minotaur is a work of fiction. Names, characters, places, and incidents either are the products of the author's imagination or are used fictitiously. Any resemblance to actual events, locales, businesses, companies, or persons, living or dead, is entirely coincidental.

Requests for permission to reprint material from this work should be sent to:

Permissions
Madville Publishing
P.O. Box 358
Lake Dallas, TX 75065

Author Photograph: Anne Day
Cover Design: Jacqueline Davis
Cover Art: *The Minotaur*, by Nick Gilley

ISBN: 978-1-948692-38-0 paperback, 978-1-948692-39-7 ebook
Library of Congress Control Number: 2020937156

To my goddess, who does have a name:

Harriet Grace

One

No one saw the white bull arrive. He was just—there!—on a white sand beach at Crete's northern shore, a silver circlet on his brow, an enormous, snorting, pawing, wholly exceptional creature, high at the shoulder as the tallest man, broad as two oxen, and of fine and classic lines despite being huge. With crescent-moon horns sharp as a double-edged labrys and his majestic sex swaying from side to side, he trotted the island, filling the roads made wide for carts bearing ollas, trampling the borders of phlomis, thyme, and crimson poppies. No hurry, no preference, no fear did he exhibit as he made his way toward the palace of Knossos, where lived the ruler of Crete, Queen Pasiphaë, and her consort, Minos.

Had the bull emerged from the sea? Was he a natural rare occurrence, a mere albino? Or was he more, much more—one of those new, male gods in animal guise?

My fellow denizens of Hades' Domain, you recently-dead 21st century souls, let us agree that no matter whence cameth the bull to the big island in the Aegean Sea, five thousand or so years ago, nor how he was transporteth to the Middle Realm, he was something else.

The most thunderstruck of Cretans, by his first sight of the bull, was Minos. Yes, *that* Minos. He's a big shot down here in Netherworld, and you newly-arrived shades are properly petrified of him—but I say again that back then, in what you moderns call the late Bronze Age, he wasn't a big shot, he was just the queen's guy.

Minos was always smart, though, and he reasoned that this

1

remarkable bull was so perfect that he was beyond the power of humankind to create, even with selective breeding. Only a god could have made such a bull. And that, to Minos, was proof—and Minos needed such proof—that Zeus and Poseidon, those male gods that he worshipped in secret, were as potent as Queen Pasiphaë's old Goddess of No Name. This bull from out of nowhere was evidence to Minos of his own godly descent from Zeus—he had asked the gods for a sign of that lineage, and then the bull had appeared! He'd always claimed that heritage but had had no evidence to back up the claim. Now he did!

He ordered tall, sturdy fences built to surround the bull in a field of garigue, burnet, and thorny broom. It was done, and the bull became a tourist attraction. Many ordinary Cretans wanted to view his perfection. And when they saw him, being dutifully religious they immediately understood that as a perfect animal the white bull must be sacrificed. Not Minos, though—oh, no, not the Big M.! Rather than lose the white one to sacrifice, Minos lofted the smoke of an hundred other sets of bovine offal to Zeus, Poseidon, Apollo, and a few lesser male gods whose benevolence he deemed relevant.

As for Queen Pasiphaë, that most beauteous, most regal of women, the high priestess of the labyrinth, when first the white bull's hooves touched the beach she awoke as from a dream of oblivion. Many times before, while in the grip of the Goddess of No Name, she had felt ecstasy, but nothing like this yearning for the beast that she sensed constantly approaching. For years she had not lain with any man, not since the days of the curse of her half-sister Circe the sorceress (of which we will have occasion to speak). But now she was deliciously unsettled. She lapsed from her daily prayer routine. Receiving reports from the corral, she did not blanch but enlarged her expectations.

On one of those blistering Aegean afternoons, Queen Pasiphaë went to the white bull's verdant setting to view him. His bright hide shimmering in sunlight, his testicles and penis casually swinging, he was more magnetically attractive than she had imagined. Desire, suppressed for years, awoke in her a lust unredeemed by love, an aching, throbbing emptiness, a yearning to be filled. Embers of it consumed Pasiphaë's sleep and troubled her waking hours until her mind knew nothing but her urgent need and the imperative to slake it. That the fire was unnatural, the object of her desire bestial, the union prohibited by Goddess and reason—only fanned the flames.

The bull was my father and Pasiphaë was my mother. I am the Minotaur.

What? I don't resemble Picasso's portrait of a minotaur? Well, any likeness that simply grafts a bull's head atop a man's torso is a simplistic reduction of my physiognomy, don't you agree? Pablo was just mirroring himself in his most animal mood. As you know, he liked to feel wicked. And I never met Picasso. How could I have? My time in the Middle Realm was, what, five hundred generations before his?

I'll bet that you former mortals from the 21st century are surprised to find that the House of Hades—that ancient dumping ground, that ultimate limbo of the dead from well before the Bronze Age—has persisted into the Internet era. But I'll also bet that you're not surprised to meet here in Netherworld such a monster as the legendary, mythological, supposedly-imaginary, wholly unrealistic, half-man, half-bull known as The Minotaur, hmm? I'll have you know that I am actually the GOAT—Greatest of All Time—of serial killers! That's the sort of personification of evil that you always thought the Hell of the ancients was for, hmm?

More likely the focus of your wondering is why *you're* here, in this ancient limbo. You think that this place cannot really be for minor sinners, and you are certain that nothing you did in the Middle Realm was bad enough to warrant your *permanent* residence here. Well, you may be right about that last part: Most of you, after your period of testing, and if you qualify—and you *will*

3

qualify if you try hard enough!—will be returning to the Middle Realm or, as you now call it, to this earth, this planet, this third rock from the sun, this Gaia. Do not doubt that your shroud is a chrysalis! You can be born again, albeit as someone else.

Really, now: Aren't you relieved not to find yourselves in some Sunday School Hell, awaiting a red-gartered Satan, demons with pitchforks, and fingernail-pulling torture? Or are you appalled that you have not entered a cloud-cushioned heaven as reward for your many good deeds? I'm sure your pluses outweighed your peccadilloes. But here we all are! And take it from me: You don't want to linger on this darkling plain. So speed your transformations! Slurp from Lethe, the River of Forgetfulness—that's the one over there, by the cypress. I prefer sips of Mnemosyne, the spring near the poplar tree yonder, although in imbibing her bittersweet waters I continually amplify my memory. Lethe is better for the likes of you. But don't overdose on her waters of forgetfulness, please, because when you depart here I want you to remember my truth. My story is a good one, and I shall tell you every scandalous bit of it. Judge Minos will not interfere— yes, that same Minos who was once ruler of Crete and is now one of our trio of judges. That's him with the serpentine tail; Dante correctly identified that characteristic. For Judge Minos my presence here is an unresolved quandary, because while it is within his authority to condemn me to the Punishment Ground, to judge me is to judge himself, and that the old bastard cannot bring himself to do.

I, Asterion, known as the Minotaur, the terror of the Aegean Seas, the undisputed master of the Cretan labyrinth, I recognize that most of you still think of me as a monster. Very un-politically-correct of you! And 'monster' is an unfortunate label, since it virtually guarantees you'll continue to judge me by improper criteria.

Of course none of *you* are monsters, or should I say none of you were monsters. No, of course not. But let me give some hard-won advice to those among you who stubbornly cling to the belief that the gods made a mistake in sending you here: Rid yourselves of the twin delusions of innocence and righteousness. Sooner or later, you'll have to! Here, willingness to acknowledge one's former appetite for evil is a reality check. To gain your release, you'll also need to admit that during your previous existence in the Middle Realm you were spoiled. Topside, none of your sins seemed irredeemable. If in the Middle Realm you went rogue, if you made a mistake, if you stumbled and strayed from the proper path, then you offered a sacrifice, or you accepted a psycho-social analysis, or you ingested a prescription drug, or you did a stint in rehab, or you uttered a felicitously worded prayer, and—presto, change-o!—horror and shame instantly vanished.

The archangel Freud was not the first to recognize the power of owning up to one's nastier desires; he was a Sigmund-come-lately to that idea.

Speaking of Freud, I must confess to you that my emergence into the Middle Realm caused the death of my mother.

I killed Mom!

There, I've said it! Now I'm free, right?

As if!

Actually, I don't *remember* killing Pasiphaë, since it happened at my birth, but I was told about it so many times that I came to accept my guilt for her death. I've even said so to her. Mom's down here too: Pasiphaë, junior daughter of Helios, that old charioteer of the sun; Pasiphaë, the high priestess of the labyrinth of Knossos and Queen of all Crete; Pasiphaë, the most gorgeous woman who ever lived. In her high priestess days, bare-breasted and wreathed in snakes, she easily incited men to perform and ladies to abandon themselves in dance. She has been in Hades' Domain long enough to have quaffed many draughts from the River of Forgetfulness, but even Lethe's liquor has not obliterated her pain. She wanders Netherworld because, it is rumored—and Hades' Hideaway outdoes Twitter and OMG in volume of gossip—that the Olympians will not yet permit her among them, although her lineage is better than most of theirs.

Down here one might have hoped that beauty counted for less. It is such an encumbrance, don't you agree? Yes, yes, I know: That's sacrilegious to say in the 21st century, the golden age of plastic surgery; but certainly the youths and maidens chosen long ago to be sacrificed through me discovered that their beauty was a problem for them—it was what got them sent to my lair to die. But—sigh, sigh—where would we be without ideals, of which beauty is the foremost?

In my youth I was taught to regard my mother with reverence and to blame myself for her death. It was only later that I blamed her for my birth.

Motherhood is incontestable: The offspring issues from a specific womb, usually under the gaze of witnesses, and apart from the very occasional baby switch there is no mistaking the link between Mom and her progeny. However, when we come to identifying Dad, uncertainty commences. Did the mother entertain more than one suitor? Whose seed took hold? Was she so drunk as to not know who gained access to her loins? Did a god have his way with her? Since back in the Bronze Age we lacked DNA evidence to ascertain paternity, we must dig deeper to find the answer to the mystery of my conception.

Behold Minos and Pasiphaë in the early strophe of their marriage: The contented couple, home and hearth aglow, clasping hands in public.

"Ain't they sweet? / The lucky love pair of Crete!"

Actually, Minos, that backwoods nobody, was fortunate to have become the consort of such a powerful female. When they met he had only recently come to a bit of prominence, having tricked his brother Sarpedon to head east and his brother Rhadamanthys to go west, which left him in sole control of what had been the bailiwick of Asterios, the nice old man who had brought up the three Zeus-begotten human sons of Europa, and who had lately—and conveniently—gone to his reward. Here's the back-story: Zeus took a liking to the Phoenician princess Europa and, assuming the form of a bull, swam with her on his back to Crete, whereupon he put his head in her lap and—wham, bam, thank you ma'am!—sired three boys. And then left her, as rapists are wont to do.

Asterios stepped in to help Europa raise those three fatherless boys, and when they were grown he brought Minos to the attention of the court. Pasiphaë fell deeply in love with the dashing young pirate, and then—despite what the older priestesses were warning her of the dangers of emotive attachments—she helped him. Talk about marrying down! To boost Minos's standing in the eyes of her subjects, Pasiphaë decreed that henceforth every Cretan must honor Minos by calling him by the appellation "husband."

There had never before been a husband. Bet you didn't know that, hmm? Prior to that moment, some two million or so days ago, men had only been impregnators, and far from the equal of women. Minos, the world's first husband—not the greatest of distinctions, hmm?

Over the course of twice nine years, Pasiphaë permitted said husband to beget upon her a passel of children, a half-dozen of whom survived infancy. Their names: Androgeos, Glaukos, Acakallis, Deione, Ariadne and Phaedra. Of several of my half-brothers and sisters I have not much to relate, for I didn't know them in the Middle Realm and by the time I arrived in Netherworld they had long since been recycled. All I learned about Number Two son, Glaukos, was that at a tender age he'd toddled away from his room, fell into a pithoi of honey, and sweetly drowned.

In the era before Minos first met Pasiphaë, when Crete's high priestesses took lovers mainly for the purpose of begetting heirs, the female offspring always became priestesses of the Goddess of No Name, and the male offspring were castrated for her service. For a thousand years that had been the drill. But Pasiphaë and Minos put a stop to it because they didn't want to neuter Androgeos, their remaining son. No more royal castration! As for their elder daughters, they continued the old tradition, betrothing Acakallis and Deione to what were touted to the girls as minor gods who lived on far-flung islands, whence they never returned, not even to show off any grandchildren. Acakallis was even linked romantically to Hermes and to Apollo. The rumor also said those male gods denied the affair, not wanting to be hit up for child support. I never met those elder sisters, neither in the Middle Realm nor in Netherworld. The younger sisters, though, Ariadne and Phaedra, were being brought up on Crete to become priestesses of the Goddess of No Name, and I came to know them well—achingly well.

But 'tis that old Goddess of whom I must now speak, that ageless, hirsute female, she of the pendulous breasts and swollen abdomen, the Goddess of the changeable seasons and of the fertile earth, she who was so self-evident that she never required—nor tolerated—a name. She had ruled forever and a day, until I came on the scene. Back then the male triumvirate of Zeus, Poseidon, and Hades were neophytes and had nothing on her, so great was her power. She moved seas, she raised islands, she brought abundance, and just as readily she swept it away.

Minos hated her. At least he did when he was a small fry, mediating in local property disputes. And here I need to clear up some old fake news: Minos as a young mediator was never the arbiter of right and wrong, for moral matters remained the province of the priestesses. Only later, after he'd hooked up with the queen, would he become the greatest potentate this side of Egypt and, after his death, a judge deemed worthy of the Supreme Bench of Netherworld. To be fair, though: In his prime in the Middle Realm, Minos was a handsome pirate admiral with a genius for shopping. Pasiphaë adored the gifts he brought to her, exotic-skinned slaves, gowns of tightly woven silk, Egyptian scarab jewels, and edible delicacies from the land of ice, pet monkeys and hoopoes.

'Twas not until after the birth of Phaedra—sort of a bonus baby—that the queen learned of her husband's infidelities. Need I add that she was the last to know? But then all the stories came out: Her man had betrayed her in every port to which he sailed, and not only with women but with nymphs and naiads, and he had done so since the beginning of their union, continuously, and without a pang of hesitation. Upon learning these facts, Pasiphaë, although deeply hurt, neither quarreled with Minos nor demanded an apology. Too queenly for that, she consulted her snakes and plotted her revenge. For it she took to the sea, accompanied by a crew of priestesses who hardly knew a mizzenmast from a poop deck. Her destination was the island Aeaea, where she importuned her half-sister, Circe the sorceress, to help her get back at the persistent philanderer.

Bad choice, Ma! Aunt Circe was no sob sister to be easily co-opted by a tale of male betrayal. It was a real no-no for Mom to claim so forcefully to Circe that they shared a father, Helios, charioteer of the sun. Circe took this plea, coming as it did from a queen whose humanity was all too evident and whose descent from Helios only gave her the power of never being cold, and treated it as a matter for play, not duty. The sorceress gave to Pasiphaë a malefic curse, to be intoned as the target ate a wicked wine-custard, whose recipe Circe also provided. Shortly, home in Crete, Pasiphaë prepared the custard, Minos ate it, she uttered the curse, and he became afflicted. Thereafter, when his passion spurted, instead of a stream of semen he ejected a noxious fluid of scorpions and millipedes, a secretion that caused the very painful death of any who dared receive it. Thus bewitched, Minos could find no paramours, and tired of purchased slave girls who writhed and died at the sure sign of his pleasure.

What a lovely revenge! Or so it initially seemed to Pasiphaë. Then she figured out the kicker in Circe's curse: that she, the queen, could not embrace Minos either, since the imprecation admitted no exceptions. And Pasiphaë's would-be lovers no longer approached her, unwilling to risk running afoul of Minos's growing power for a go-around with a middle-aged matron.

Impenetrable, stone, joyless, Minos and Pasiphaë waged open domestic warfare in the palace. "The olive jars leak." "The snakes are shedding." "The water-closet stinks." "There's not enough treasure in the treasury." "My lineage is more godly than yours." Ah, that last contention was a fine field for battle!

"If you're so divine, Minos, how could a mere sorceress like Circe have vexed you? Where is the proof of your descent from Zeus? Europa was just an ordinary woman with three bastard sons, who were rescued from pauperism by that nice old man, Asterios."

Pasiphaë whispered her doubts about Minos's descent to every courtier at the palace and to every supplicant who approached the temple, until Minos realized that even if he killed the queen the secret scorn of the islanders would not fade. It was only then that Minos reasoned he could silence them all, and wrest true power from Pasiphaë, by definitively proving his descent from Zeus. And so he prayed to the triumvirate of male gods to give him a sign of his true lineage.

Instanter, the white bull appeared on the Cretan shore.

Pasiphaë waited until the night of the first full moon after the bull had been penned in its field. Oiling and perfuming herself with sandalwood and lavender, she then, alone, terrified yet compelled, climbed the rails into the fenced field and edged toward the bull. He gazed in her direction, and then trotted away to mount one of his bovine harem.

Pasiphaë sacrificed her rival. She replaced her own perfume with the dead cow's odor of dung, milk, grass, and sweat, and so spiced, presented her rump. Again the bull disdained her.

"Father Helios, aid me!"—but the ensuing morning was full of clouds and Helios was obscured. She returned to the temple. "Goddess of No Name, forgive me for having momentarily forgotten you, the spiritual center of my life. Grant me the relief I seek!"—but the positions of the snakes on the tiles revealed nothing. Her ache did not abate; it increased ninefold.

Pasiphaë sought out Daedalus—yes, *that* Daedalus, the smith who would eventually make wings for himself and his son Icarus. But I'm getting ahead of my story. Daedalus was on Crete because Pasiphaë had given him sanctuary after an unfortunate incident elsewhere (of which we will also have occasion to speak). He had become one of the queen's many slaves, and she had honored him by not forcing him to become a eunuch. Rather, she had rewarded his usefulness by allotting to him a wife whose name and origin was the island Cyclade. The artificer's main task was fashioning additional chambers in the labyrinth; and at the queen's command he also hammered and forged armor for Minos, and toys to delight the royal couple's children, and gadgets to make life in the palace more comfortable.

"Daedalus, my jewel! I demand a device, an accommodation, a rack for more than torture, an apparatus to trick the bull into believing I am a cow."

"No, my queen."

Few had ever previously refused the high priestess of Crete and survived, yet change was in the air: men were rising in status, although they had not yet become the equal of women. And Daedalus was wary because successful manufacture of a device to fulfill the queen would surely earn him the displeasure of Minos, which would lead to pain, deprivation, torture, and a lingering death—Minos-the-pirate's predilection for what we now call sadism was already the gossip of the Aegean Seas.

"Sorry, my lady."

"Helios will maintain your smithy's fire so that it will never die; you'll no longer have to haul wood to stoke it. Circe will enhance the features of your toys; they'll dance as humans do. Beyond that, I'll be yours for the asking. Yes! It is you, Daedalus, whom I truly desire! Once I have scratched this itch for the bull, I'll devote my life and riches to your pleasure."

"I am honored but nonetheless must decline."

"Fool! I'll have Cyclade flayed alive in front of your eyes. Icarus, your beloved child, will be shackled and sold to the Lycians and subjected to the unspeakable practices of the East!"

Daedalus was silent.

"You are intimidated by the task. Your refusal is cowardice, is failure of the imagination, is acknowledgement that your talent is unfit to meet this supreme challenge. I can no longer doubt that your best work has been done by apprentices. You are not the greatest artificer, the rival of the gods! Truth is, you're mediocre!"

It is always pride, isn't it? Arrogant, blind, unreasoning pride: not a one of us so placid that we do not perk up when thusly pricked. I'm certain that some among you recently-arrived souls have been whisked to Netherworld as a consequence of dying in the process of committing deeds when your pride was similarly wounded and stimulated. Well, you're in good company! Without pride, you say, we humans would accomplish nothing. Bah! Is the scorpion proud of his sting? Does a tree have pride? Does one of heaven's stars?

"Your highness," Daedalus bowed, a fortnight later, displaying his models to the queen, "I have produced a half-dozen exemplars of bovine seductiveness among which you may choose: The smoldering, the coy, the innocent, the motherly, the punishing, and the inevitable. Which would you like?"

"Combine them all—if such a feat is not beyond your competence."

On the night of the next full moon, Daedalus's combinant machine was ready, and it was a wonder: a waving tail, slow-moving haunches, a smooth hide, and a mechanism that allowed the torso to yield while providing support for the driving force of the bull. Pasiphaë crawled inside the faux-cow and lay prone, her eyes gazing at the dull green heath, her arms clenching supports, her legs spread, her loins oiled, and her mind primed with potions so she could endure the pain of penetration.

The acrid scent of heat, the warning snort, the earth trembling under his tread: Each she had imagined so many times that when they came to pass each was a paroxysm of concurrence with her fantasy. More swiftly than she had believed possible, the bull mounted and she and he were one.

By human standards, the copulation of animals seems unbearably brief. By animal standards, I can reliably inform you, the copulation of humans—lacks intensity.

For Pasiphaë, lying there coupled to the bull, time became

irrelevant, consciousness an encumbrance, and the gods—at last!—knowable.

Days later she awoke, on a solitary straw pallet in the labyrinth's holiest chamber, able to remember neither the ache of her lust nor any sense of fulfillment. Battered and exhausted, her loins torn, her voice reduced to a whisper by the strain of screams she did not recall making, she was in a stupor for an entire week before asking for food. By then she knew that life had quickened within.

The palace's eunuch physician, Enteros, came to the labyrinth and was blindfolded and escorted to the queen's lying-in space. He put his ear to her belly and heard my heart beat.

"Return to the palace, physician. Pregnancy is a woman's concern, and will be in the hands of the priestesses. I no longer wish to have males around me, even those without testicles. From this day forth, the temple is closed to men."

Pasiphaë also shunted aside Daedalus, to whom she had made promises of adultery and insurrection. Rather wisely, the still-orchidate artificer did not press for payment for services rendered.

The priestesses agreed with Pasiphaë that her coupling with the bull had been remarkable. Just as astounding was that desire had left her as though blown away by a summer storm; this was proof, they said, that her obsession had been induced by the Goddess. They threw the snakes. All that could be definitively concluded from their positions on the tiles was that Pasiphaë was blessed among women, and would become the mother of some sort of divine or semi-divine being.

She accepted the diagnosis.

As her burden enlarged, she became more radiant and calm. White doves flew to her hair and made a living crown. On the day of the summer solstice, holding the hands of her daughters Ariadne and Phaedra, she led a distaff-only procession up Mount Jutkas, whose peaks are the sleeping profile of the face of the Goddess of No Name. Alongside the path crowds genuflected before Pasiphaë's march, and women who had initially just paused in their work to catch a glimpse of her cast aside what they were doing and joined the procession. Dancing, chanting, chewing on the dangerously narcotic leaves of the crocus and nipping at the holy wine, the pregnant queen and followers wound their way up the modest heights to a point overlooking the sea. At the shrine, Pasiphaë poured holy wine, oil, and honey until the libation basins were awash with sweet syrups that sluiced down the mountain and brought lions prowling to their source. Pasiphaë commanded the beasts, and the lions meekly sniffed at her burgeoning belly. In their presence, she anointed Ariadne and Phaedra in the mysteries of the cult and raised consecrated smoke.

In the palace, Minos—so publicly cuckolded—mulled over his three dilemmas: What to do with Pasiphaë, what to do with Daedalus, and what do to with the bull. He wished to kill all three, but was mature enough to stifle his rage. To harm Pasiphaë would spur revolt and would anger the ancient goddess, and although Minos was furious at Daedalus, he knew he would be better served by not impairing the artificer's future usefulness.

The white bull from the sea, however, was another matter. The bull had twice proved Minos's own godly descent, once by his appearance and a second time by mounting Pasiphaë, which reflected the interest of Zeus and his brother, Poseidon. Such attention from a god was always an honor, but it did not erase the king's deepening anger at the bull.

After the mating, the white stud had been running rampant through the island, stampeding herds through planted fields and ravaging villages. Minos wanted him captured, and awarded the task to Androgeos, the finest athlete that our island had ever produced. Minos had previously confided to Andro his plans to seize rulership of the island from the womenfolk, but hadn't been able to predict when that would happen. For Andro, a young man in his prime, the thought of waiting many years for his turn on the throne was unbearable. He longed for something to conquer now, and Minos gave him the task:

14

"Capture the ravisher—alive—my son. If you succeed, you shall command the greatest fleet ever assembled."

My brother took many men with long spears. They followed the trail of destruction and soon surrounded the white bull. Androgeos then squared to face alone the formidable creature. He ran at the bull and leapt up between the horns. For anyone else, this would have been suicidal, but he grasped the horns as handholds to facilitate his somersault to the hindquarters. Reaching that precarious post, he then slung his hobble about the beast's feet and brought him crashing to the ground. Shortly thereafter, Androgeos and his retinue of mighty warriors, carrying on the long poles of their spears the trussed, upside down, bawling bull, entered the labyrinth and went through to the grand, high-vaulted court.

With great and pious pomp, the priestesses splayed the white bull out on an iron grill suspended over the tiled marble floor, and surrounded him with all the trappings of glory: incense, libations, and song. Everyone from the nobility then came into the hall to see him, led by Minos and Pasiphaë. Her obvious pregnancy evoked much comment. My mother knew it would be her last public appearance. She consecrated the bull and Minos stuck in the first knife. An anguished roar escaped the bovine impregnator. Then the priestesses, their courage gallantly to the fore, thrust in their own, jeweled knives. Geysers of blood cascaded over the upper classes as they jostled for position under the sacred shower. Slowly, the grating was lowered toward the tiles, where the unarmed crowd performed the holy rites of *sparagmos* and *omophagia*, using their teeth and nails to rip away morsels of the immobilized, dying bull, and eating the morsels until there was nothing left on the iron rack but bones. The skull and horns were presented to Minos, who held them high while he and Pasiphaë recited the ceremony's closing prayers. A hosanna was on everyone's lips and a piece of the bull was in everyone's gullet.

Thus perished my father.

After the obliteration of the white bull, Minos tried to atone for his arrogance in having summoned the sign from Poseidon and Zeus; and a repentant Pasiphaë tried to atone for placing Circe's curse on him. But though the royal couple had gotten beyond their mutual hate, there was neither time nor spiritual energy enough to make real amends.

Pasiphaë's body swelled. She understood that her burden would be too large to be born without damaging her. She believed that the Goddess of No Name would not allow her to perish in childbirth, but advised Ariadne and Phaedra—the latter, too young to comprehend—that in the event of her death they should seek the protection of Androgeos and the counsel of Daedalus, and to comport themselves as grand-daughters of Helios. The pains tightened into a girdle of iron.

Death and birth approached simultaneously.

Pasiphaë screamed as my emerging head ripped her asunder, tore the length and breadth of her sex until she, too, drained of blood, whitened, and died.

Thus perished my mother.

As all dead humans must, Pasiphaë saw Hermes the messenger god hover in the air and irresistibly summon her onward. So saddened was Hermes that he did not wait for the proper ceremony to have been held but appeared before her at the moment of her death and quickly led her to the black poplar. Thus when they reached the edge of Netherworld and Pasiphaë climbed into the ferry to cross the Styx, she wore not the royal green raiment of queenly burial but the blood-stained gossamer birthing gown, the bright scarlet liquid not yet dry. Charon the ferryman of the Styx, equally as saddened as Hermes, did not insist on his usual coin before allowing her a place in his craft, and Cerberus, the dog with three heads who guards the gates, did not even growl at her approach to our domain's shores, for such a death as Pasiphaë's is holy, and commands the respect of all the gods and their creatures.

Two

The servants charged by Minos with the task of exposing me to my death bungled the job: not willing to trudge all the way up Mount Jutkas, they jettisoned me on a lesser hillside. Guys, I thank you for your laziness! My more sincere kudos to the lioness of Jutkas who found me—directed, I have no doubt, by the Goddess of No Name—and who carried me in her jaws to a field close to the palace and deposited me near a herd of those who looked most like me, the palace's cattle.

The cows' fulsome udders proved spectacularly hospitable to my semi-cloven little hands and grasping mouth. Talk about your idyllic childhoods! For a moon I swung from teat to teat, blissfully unaware of aught but instant gratification. A hillside of aromatic heath and spurges brightened with crocuses and lilies, a grassy lea rustling with the busywork of beetles and cicadas, the occasional olive and palm and an ancient cypress for midday shade, a stream running clear and mellifluous, the ocean's distant sigh, the burred tips of the mountains: Marvelous!

There, for me, Meat was a concept that did not exist.

Are you surprised that I was originally a vegan? Puh-lease! Acknowledge my early innocence of blood. All I knew was bovinity: The herd was hungry and my stomach growled; the herd needed to move on and my hooves were impelled; the herd was happy and my bellow charmed the moon.

From the cows—the bulls had very little to do with me—I learned patience and equanimity, which you will agree are virtues that in the 21st century have gone out of style. Most of you newly-arrived shades entirely lack both.

17

They will write no songs about Rheo, my surrogate mother, but she was a wonderful cow—stolid, kind, strict when necessary, forgiving, and compliant without being complaisant. For me her udder was always full, her tongue warm, her philosophy serviceable. "Don't butt life and it won't butt you." "Enjoy the sunshine, enjoy the rain that relieves the sunshine, enjoy the salt that makes you thirsty and enjoy the stream that quenches your thirst." "Count the stars before venting your anger; count nothing before venturing your love." To Rheo, life was bountiful: Cows had more milk than needed to suckle their own calves, and the wastrel bulls more semen than required to impregnate a single cow—and so it made sense for bulls to cover an entire harem, and for cows' milk to be drawn off by lactally-challenged humans. It also made sense for cows to occupy the high moral ground—ours was near the cedars and carobs—and to perpetuate the race. Rheo asked only to be cherished, and when the *notia* came, for her death to be swift.

The pheromes of the notia, an acrid, salty, eye-stinging wind, announced that a death was occurring. You smelled it coming from the mountain when the lioness took her prey, and from the ocean when the fishermen returned with the catch of the day. And we in the herd were also used to a certain telltale prefiguring: A human herdsman would appear among us, put a vine around the neck of a cow, and lead her away. That was prelude to our shortly smelling the notia, and to knowing that she would never return to us alive. We would pledge that she should continue to exist in our herd's collective memory.

I cropped burnet and rockrose, thyme and garigue, unaware that my birth had set in motion such a complete disgrace of my late mother, Pasiphaë, that Minos was soon able to shutter the locus of her power, the labyrinth, and to demand that the islanders call him 'king.' On Crete there had never before been a king; previously, the island's topmost ruler had been the chief priestess. While the Hellenes, Babylonians, and Lydians had

had kings as rulers, the title had never before been applicable in Crete. I would later come to understand that 'king' meant he-who-is-by-birth-or-conquest-in-charge, sort of like one of those new, male gods who were trying to usurp power from the Goddess of No Name, whom even my herd prayed to.

Because the cows and bulls of that herd had been treating me as a fellow bovine, I had no sense that my physical structure was unusual until several moons had waxed and waned. By then I had grown considerably, and one day I advanced further into a pool than I ever had, and saw a reflection of my rump, naked of fur. I galloped crying to Rheo, who comforted me by explaining that my differences just meant that I was special.

Shortly, and for the first time, I experienced an urge to rise up on my hind limbs, if only to see further. I practiced until I was comfortable on those hind two. When the human herdsmen noticed this, they ran in the direction of the notia and soon returned in company of two humans of female aroma, who upon seeing me made astonished and fearful noises. The larger human female exuded a scent of intense floral warmth, and had a black mane, and knobby nipples—lovely, though inadequate by bovine standards. I allowed her to scratch behind my ears. Thus was I introduced to my human sister Ariadne. She was then thirteen and the smaller female, my other sister, Phaedra, but eight. They were already opposites—Ariadne dark-tressed, warm and daring, Phaedra golden-haired, rather cool and self-contained.

Unlike cows and bulls, humans seemed to articulate thoughts mainly with the voice, augmented by hand and facial gestures. They did not use licking, stance, odors, horn digs, ear positions, tail wavings, cropping patterns, defecation or urination to communicate. How could they convey subtlety of emotion?

Little Phaedra began to dash about the field and so did I, but when I came too close I frightened her and she leapt into the arms of a male human who had just arrived. He was imposing, tall and muscular, with a black beard to match his black hide-coverings and a feral scent. He handed Phaedra to a herdsman and crouched to face me.

Blackbeard was a skilled adversary, knocking me off my feet, twisting my limbs to the point of pain. I struggled valiantly but could not toss him, and he soon had a knee on my chest and was reaching into his tunic for a gleaming stick. I heard Ariadne scream something, over and over, until I had listened to it enough to repeat it myself.

"No. Don't kill him. No!" I said.

He stepped back, allowing me to roll away and right myself. Thus was I introduced to my brother Androgeos.

Over the course of the next half moon, my human visitors came daily to the field to play and instruct me. Tag, tumble, jump, chase, and tickle alternated with lessons on the subjunctive, the ablative, and the intransitive.

I learned that Andro, Ariadne, and Phaedra were not only royalty but actually family of mine, that we shared a mother, unfortunately now deceased. Nothing was said to me, just then, of my having caused the queen's death, but I was given to understand that I owed my continued existence to Minos's decision to spare me.

It was the smart move: The king understood that my survival to date must owe to the gods having allowed it, and reasoned that if he now executed me the gods would surely visit upon him unimaginable catastrophes. So Minos permitted me to live and, from afar, bestowed on me the name of Asterion. Star-born I was not, yet the name rang comfortably in my ears. Each day at dusk, when my human siblings departed the meadow I felt a yearning to accompany them to the Great Inside. I dreamed that to spend the sunless period with them would be enjoyable, and that it would be easy to return to Rheo's side the next morning.

Sooner recover virginity than relinquish the palace for the field! But then, no seeker after experience ever properly values the safety of his state of ignorance.

"Do not suffer the hobble, for the yoke follows," Rheo counseled as I spent more and more time each day with the humans. "Respect the elders for their wisdom, and not only because they have the largest horns." Nonetheless, one evening at dusk I trotted off in the direction of the palace, in company of my human family. As we approached the entrance, surrounded by flowers of amazing variety, color, and scent, I reared onto my hind legs to walk as they did into their domain.

The doors shut behind us. I was immediately uneasy. Never before had there been limits to my horizons. Now the ground extended up and over and around me! I beheld approaching a male human of approximate size to Androgeos but of greater bulk and grayer mane, his body covered in the purple tinges of sunset, his emanations clear, sharp, and warning, his person flanked by servants. I sighed. Here, at last, was the obviously dominant male of the human herd. His implacable stare, his air of expecting obeisance—small chance he'd allow any other guy access to his harem, or suffer any female to order him around!

"Speak, Asterion," King Minos commanded.

"King Minos have big testicles?"

A shocked hush fell over the company, followed by a huge peal of laughter from the king, in which the rest of the family and court then joined.

I shall not tarry over the embarrassment of my toilet training. Or my introduction to new edible delicacies and consequent diarrhea. Or my distress at understanding how different I was from those who were entirely human.

The nobles and servants at the palace ignored me. Only the gimpy Daedalus spoke to me regularly and kindly. Minos had asked him to design something to cover my nakedness, and during the fittings we conversed. I asked if he had a mate.

"My wife Cyclade. Currently she has the sweats, the chills, the aches, the numbness, and only ventures from her pallet to relieve herself."

"The herd uses the crushed seeds of the barberry bush for

21

that. But if Cyclade's illness never worsens or lessens, Rheo would say she hurts because her special cud-chewing space is unavailable."

"Rheo is correct: Cyclade is a priestess of the Goddess, and the labyrinth has been closed. Minos has instead decreed worship of Zeus and Apollo."

"What is 'worship?'"

"What we humans do to make sure that the gods will not harm us—present offerings, say good things about them, and make sure not to transgress their rules."

"Like I have to do with Minos?"

One of my duties was to sit at the king's feet in the judgment chamber. Sometimes he would pet me and call me his "minitaur." As often, he'd lecture me. "Power, Asterion," he liked to say, "power is the ability to make people do what they would otherwise resist doing. Most people are slothful and unimaginative. They act only when compelled by hunger, fear, lust, the need for attention, or because someone else forces them to. Yes, Daedalus, what d'you want?"

"For the palace cistern, your highness: the drawing-well—enclosed or open?"

"Enclosed. Dismissed! There, Asterion: now Daedalus will go and forge a beautiful grate, and think up an ingenious way of attaching it to the well. Power systematizes the formless; power extracts order from chaos; power provides meaning to life."

In Minos's forum judgments, I noticed patterns. The king routinely gave to the handsome and took away from the ugly. He awarded fields and hearths to groups represented by men while wresting homesteads from groups led by women. I repeated these observations to my sister, Ariadne, one evening as we sat in her bedroom, looking out at Knossos. I asked whether Minos really did not like females.

"Of course! He owes everything he is to women." She was perched on her enormous bed, dressed in a white tunic, legs crossed demurely. "Many nights I sit here and gaze at the lit candles in the windows of the city. Knossos is a huge candelabrum until people grow sleepy and cap the candles. When one window of candles is put out, very soon afterwards the neighboring window goes dark, and the rest follow. And the next night, if people snuff their candles earlier, others do the same and the darkness arrives more quickly. But if some people kept their candles lit, others would too, and there would never be complete darkness."

"You are already a high priestess, sister of mine."

"No, I'm still a virgin."

She announced that when she did become a high priestess she would restore the labyrinth to its proper glory and once more direct the homage of the peoples of the Cycladean Seas toward the Goddess of No Name. "Androgeos is with us," she whispered. "When he becomes king, he'll open the labyrinth for me and we'll jointly rule. Will you be part of the plan, Asterion?"

"You could have asked me to impale myself on my horns and I would have done it. Moreover, what you request of me—company on an adventure—seems well within my capability. I shall become sovereign of the fields, protector of Rheo and the herd, interlocutor between the human and the bovine, charged with bringing the mammalian races into closer harmony."

Was Ariadne's plan just a teenage fantasy? Unlike most juvenilia, it was specific and it did not predicate its success on too many things happening precisely as anticipated. We did not seek universal peace, just on our island; we did not insist on equality for man, woman, and beast, just an accommodation for mutual benefit. "Can Icky be a prince?" Phaedra wanted to know. Icarus, only child of Daedalus, was her age and equally as spoiled—the two blonde tykes roamed the palace shrieking with delight, terrorizing the servants. Daedalus also knew of Ariadne's notion, but had not yet joined the Dream Team.

Minos had already found out about her plans. "I'm glad little Ariadne's mind is active," Minos said to me in the royal chamber. He snacked on roast turtledove wings, I on braised rose petals with sesame seeds. "Let her snakes writhe and signify. To compel Ariadne to abandon her schemes now would only strengthen her resolve. As she reaches womanhood and becomes subject to other desires, her faith in illusory realms will atrophy. It's Andro I must pay more attention to."

The king realized that he could no longer satisfy Androgeos by promises of the largest fleet ever assembled. Since that fleet was almost ready, Minos now had to get him to sail away with it before Andro figured out that such a massive fleet could as easily be used to conquer Crete as some far-flung state. So Minos whetted Andro's appetite for battle by telling him that the Athens tyrant, Aegeus, would be holding games to determine the best athletes of the world, and would of course expect his own Athenians to be the champions.

"Has he never heard of the greatest bull-leaper of Crete?" Androgeos said. "I've already outrun, outleaped, and out-thrown every able man on Crete, including your eunuchs, whose muscular development makes up for their lack of testicles."

"Wanna wrestle me again, big bro?"

Not many moons since, Androgeos had toppled me without difficulty, but now I was taller than he and my horns extended wide enough to make walkers in the palace halls cling to the walls lest during my passage I nick them.

One overcast day, clad in loincloths, Androgeos and I faced off in the palace's largest chamber, before an audience of Minos, Ariadne, and the court. This time Andro had no hobbles or knives, and my horn-tips were cushioned. He dove for my legs and toppled me but I twisted away and soon realized that my greater weight and strength would eventually enable me to pin him and keep him pinned. But were I to best Androgeos, what would ensue? Humiliated, he might have a temper tantrum and refuse to go on his trip, which would ruin Ariadne's plans. On the other horn, given my decided advantages, were I to lose, Ariadne might reverse her evaluation of my worth and decide that I was not really fit to be the future lord of the Great Outdoors. To achieve my goals, then, required a long, slow, arduous fight to a draw. I made the clash last long enough to permit Andro to feel he'd kept his honor, and only then acceded to Ariadne's suggestion that we stop fighting. 'Twas a famous non-victory.

Preparations for Androgeos' sailing were nearly complete. He would journey to Athens by a roundabout sea route, during which he could hone his ability to plunder and whet his appetite for pleasure. At Athens, his fleet's potency would also ensure Androgeos a respectful reception.

"Don't go to the port, Asterion," Ariadne pleaded with me on the morning of his departure. "You'll frighten people who don't know what you look like, and even if you don't frighten them you'll make them look at you rather than Andro on his big day." I bowed to her request. The time would be perfect for exploring the palace. Amazing, isn't it, how even as we congratulate ourselves for never taking orders, we provide ourselves with reasons to obey?

Roaming, I meandered through the private rooms. In Ariadne's windowed suite the snakes lay in torpor in their painted box and her bed was strewn with body paints and discarded skirts. I bent over the bed and inhaled the intoxicating smells, then sat on the covers to separate from among them the spoor of her bodily excitement. Whilst I rolled my mane in these rapturous essences, Kharo appeared in the doorway. A mature noblewoman, tall, full-bodied, with a high rump that seemed about to burst its coverings, she had evidently followed me, for she showed no surprise and approached the bed at an angle that would intercept any attempt on my part to flee. She walked toward me, untying one by one the many bows of her bodice-jacket and bell skirt. Scents of desire, warmth and urgency assailed my nostrils, awakening in me a strange sensation. "At the wrestling match," Kharo said, "I began by watching my lover, the young prince; but as the day wore on my gaze inexorably shifted to you."

As she continued to untie the bows, an urge to thrust into her besieged my brain. I had no idea what to expect when she guided my penis into a warm, wet, salty, previously hidden place in her loins. Entrance suffused me with pleasure and welcome.

I felt a sense of rightness: this was my proper environment, my best occupation. I sought to burrow deeper. My thrusts increased in pace. Kharo gasped. Her face contorted.

"Are you in pain?"

"Don't stop, Asterion!"

Enthusiasm took me over and I knew with great certitude what I wanted to do and I did it and did it and was still doing it with great gusto when Kharo bucked and her flesh that surrounded my penis overflowed with warmth and wetness and she dug her fingernails into my mane and clung closer and moaned as at the base of my tail a new sensation began and spread up my backbone and down my legs and my body thrilled and my mind expanded to cover the universe.

If this was what sexual congress was all about, why did humans ever waste their time doing anything else?

Kharo cried, then insisted that the tears stemmed not from sadness but from happiness. How very odd! Joyous tears. Pleasurable pain. Release from the mind as the body asserted itself. What peculiar glory you humans prize.

Over the next hours I learned that the sources of hedonistic delight were many and varied. Kharo confided that she had expected to be in control of this coupling, and was not but was nonetheless thrilled. I paid no attention as sunlight gave way to fuliginous shadows and the wind brought in the faint sounds of the returning procession.

A pack of noblemen discovered us. Among them was an old man called Patroclus, whom I recognized as Kharo's husband. He started to attack me. I couldn't understand why—clearly, if his female had so willingly approached me for sex, she did not belong exclusively to him. Moreover, no self-respecting bull would fight another bull *after* a mounting; such contests took place in *advance*, with mating as the prize! Yet sword in one hand, dagger in the other, Patroclus assailed me among the rumpled bed coverings and discarded clothes. It was the world's first true bullfight—although the matador didn't wear tight-fitting pants or stuff his codpiece.

Among the gathering crowd I searched for Ariadne, but she was not there, nor was Minos.

The men with double-axes made no move to restrain Patroclus. All expected him to kill me. Sword to the fore, Patroclus committed to a charge and I swung my horns and knocked away his arm, although not before he slashed my withers. Blood flowed over the matted mane of my chest—another new sensation for me. It hardly hurt or slowed me, but the sight, smell, and flow of blood made me realize that in this fight it would not be enough to merely deflect Patroclus—he would not desist until he was dead. What a pathetic matador! On his next approach, I swept the sword from him with one horn and, swinging back with the other, gored his belly. I had never before ripped through anything, and was amazed at how swiftly a horn bit in and produced a geyser of blood. He remained impaled, so I shook my body to rid it of the burden, and almost inadvertently tore him apart. His intestines spilled out with the bodily juices—and I instantly smelled the notia. I cut at him with teeth and hooves, seeking to scatter to the winds he who caused me pain just when I'd been feeling pretty good about myself.

Labrys bearers beat me from the dying man. One's ax took a slice from my leg. I lurched back and away. Ariadne's intercession halted them. I turned my attention to staunching with a rumpled bed sheet the flow of blood from my left leg. Tears etched black lines from Ariadne's eyes down her rouged cheeks, and I fancied that she was both disappointed that my bestial nature had asserted itself—for such was the judgment of the crowd—and chagrined that for my sexual awakening I had not chosen her. Shortly, King Minos arrived to view the carnage. He instructed his soldiers to gather the remains of Patroclus and directed the older priestesses to prepare the pieces of the dead man for an honored burial. Minos's commands left no space to cavil; I had seldom seen him so breathtakingly regal.

Glances from the retreating noblewomen told me that had Kharo not seduced me that day, another of them would have done so the next day. And had I not gored the hapless Patroclus, some other man would soon have provoked me to kill him.

A rumbling, rattling noise came from the corridor outside the bedchamber. Moments later an openwork iron cage arrived on a wheeled cart, guided by Daedalus, who slid open its grate. "Please get in, Asterion." His voice was gentle. "Now we are similarly impaired," he said as I hobbled into the cage. In that abattoir of a bedchamber, only Daedalus acknowledged that I was still the creature he had known in earlier moons. The barred grate was firmly closed behind me, and then, more so than ever before, I was Inside.

Enteros, the eunuch physician, took pleasure in applying fiery pitch from a torch to my bloodied leg until I screamed with pain and passed into sleep. When I awoke, the cage and I were in a windowless room, under the gaze of six sentinel ax-wielders. A chamber pot awaited, and there was a low dish meant for food, although it was currently empty.

A day and a night passed amid fitful periods of wakefulness. Sounds of ceremony came through doors: I must not be far from the king's reception hall. Why did the king not feed me, since he had allowed Enteros to prevent my bleeding to death? My hunger grew. On the evening of the third day a few scraps were thrown near enough to the cage so that I could reach them. I avidly thrust them into my mouth. The taste soon told me what they were: Meat.

Ah, my fellow denizens of Hades' depths, you 21st centurions are way ahead of me, aren't you? More quickly than I did five thousand years ago, you understand that Minos was training me on cooked Meat, and would shortly lead me to eat raw Meat and not to mind if it came from a human being. As I devoured those first orts, should I have known toward what savagery I was heading, and therefore refused to eat? You, of course, would have kept your mouth shut, hmm?

Listen up: My true choice was between finding a way to go on, regardless of where it might lead, or dying. I determined

28

not to die then, nor there, and never by the hand of Minos. I. Chose. Life.

A continuous procession of Cretans filed into the chamber in which I sat in my cage, to stare at me for a while and then exit. Some trembled in fear, a few genuflected, and many brought offerings. Oil, candles, grain, recently slain lambs and other edibles were placed on the low table, near enough for me to smell and see but out of reach—a special torment to one being deliberately starved. Some gawkers in the daily line spoke to me. I mostly kept silent. However, on one occasion a terrible hurt seared through my leg and I roared. A moment later the earth trembled.

In the field, such tremors seemed no more than a rustling of the soil. In the palace, the shimmering shudder knocked offerings from the table and forced stumbles from the ax-bearers—one accidentally lopped off a visitor's arm. The conjunction of my roar and the earth's movement were noted; thereafter the quantity and opulence of the oblations kicked up a notch, as visitors no longer considered me as less than human, but as more than human. As a god?

How absurd! A god would not permit himself to be caged. Yet I was receiving homage fit for a god: mothers urged their newborns to gaze upon me, young couples knelt expectantly for a blessing, and rheumy-eyed elders stared at me to fix my image in their minds before embarking on their journeys through death. What wretched lives you humans lead!

To recover from my amazement at being treated like a god yet being in a cage, I attempted what you moderns call meditation. It was a suspension I'd learned in the field, where we in the herd spent whole afternoons in sweet lethargy, unmoving though aware. Your heartbeat matches the rhythm of the clouds, you experience the tickle of the grass and the paths of the busy insects beneath your stomachs, and the soft wind as it rustles your hide and whispers in your ears of faraway meadows, you hear the faint aromatic shout of flowers, feel the subtle transformations of the sky and its echoes in your own digestive tract.

In the cage I practiced that stillness to resist the impulse to rise up and destroy everything around me, including myself. My hunger continued, even though little Phaedra and Icarus brought me sweets, convinced that I was still their companion of grassy gambols. Daedalus too made regular stops, ostensibly to test whether the cage was holding. As he gave me advice on exercising an injured leg, he moved his hands from joint to joint on the metal bars, tracing the iron seals. Each visit, his fingers followed the same route.

One day he thrilled me by a whisper: "Stay awake tonight."

At an hour when the palace hung motionless and mute in the salty air, a black-robed, blackmaned figure glided into the torchlit chamber, her face aglow with colors in the mode of the Goddess, her nubile body glistening under the weight of necklaces, bracelets and earrings, her musk redolent and alluring. Ariadne gave small gifts to the six guards so she could approach the cage alone. She sat on the low table and held out her ringed hand for me to kiss.

"Do not give way to lethargy and despair, Asterion. Marshal your strength and resolve toward Androgeos's return." She gave me to understand, in a whisper, that our reunion and triumph would depend upon the death of the king.

"Do you expect me to kill him? I won't. An animal kills only for food, not for political gain."

"Regicide will be Androgeos' task."

She vanished just before the blue-green dawn, but the image of her black-framed glory insinuated its way into my fantasies, supplanting Kharo's as the discrete object of my desire.

A moon later, as I sat staring at the slow-moving line of supplicants, a commotion arose—shouting and scurrying that resulted in the abrupt dismissal of the procession from my chamber, and in the daylight entrance of my sister. Her garments hastily arranged, her demeanor distraught, Ariadne was once more the teenaged girl.

"Androgeos is dead. In Athens. We can't tell, really, how he died. The body, his body—so awful, Asterion!—distorted; I could hardly bear to look."

I was jealous that any other being could spark such thunderous emotion from her, but I calmed myself and tried to elicit the tale of my brother's demise. As told to her by the sailors, it was this: After a successfully rapacious tour of the Cycladean islands and the Peloponnesian coastal cities, Androgeos and crew arrived in the Bay of Phaleron at Piraeus, anchored out of arrow range, and climbed the hills to Athens. King Aegeus offered them wine, women, and song. As Andro practiced his running, leaping, and hurling, it became obvious to onlookers that he would surely win the laurels. On the first day, he placed second in the running competition, and the next day he easily won the leaping. On the third day, a Mycenaen discus thrower's missile "accidentally" struck Androgeos in the head. My brother ran in crazed circles until he dropped and died. King Aegeus imprisoned the discus thrower. But the Cretans, as they sailed home with Androgeos's body, could not avoid concluding that my brother's death, however inadvertent it had appeared, was Aegeus's doing.

"Far greater hurts await us all, my sister," I said. "You are young, beautiful, and smart. Feel grief for the passage of the notia over our brother, and honor him with your tears—but do not yield to sorrow, for if you do we will not prevail."

After the announcement of Andro's death, the processional line through my chamber did not reappear, and Daedalus seemed exhausted as he moved his hands over the bars; he mumbled about completing extra work on the labyrinth. The next night, in a light sleep, I became aware of a presence near the chamber, one that wanted to speak but could not. By the time I roused from torpor, the king was gone.

A week after the news of Androgeos's death, only five of six eunuchs appeared after a shift change. In the nearby tribunal chamber, voices were raised, and then I heard the stomp of a cudgel on the floor, followed by an anguished wail and the opening and closing of a distant door. A bit later, there was the scent of the notia, and at dusk the guards brought me a platter of cut-up raw.Meat and bones. Although the smallness of the pieces disguised the origin, I knew that it was the man who had been killed by the sixth guard.

I had conquered space, fought time to a standstill, and was reaching beyond hope and despair. My future stretched before me, a yawning abyss. But, racked by hunger, and even as I knew that slaking that hunger would seal my fate, I ate my supper.

Once Minos had proved that I would, indeed, eat recently dead human flesh, he had the cage and me trundled out of the palace.

For a brief moment, I again experienced the Great Outdoors—the sun bright and warm, the air suffused with floral essences and the far-off sounds of sea and forests. On the next hill the unmistakable shape of Rheo swished her tail in recognition, a sight that gladdened and saddened me. I bellowed a goodbye to her; the guards trembled, thinking my roar foretold an earthquake.

Ahead of me loomed the labyrinth's great door, which had been opened. The grate of my cage was set carefully next to the door of the labyrinth and opened. The guards' double-axes goaded me from one space into the other, and the door closed behind me.

Thus did I enter the world's entrails, the defile of dreams, the greatest of all Insides; like a babe reversing the journey of his birth, I pierced into the temple of my tormented mother.

Three

With lowered head and horns I repeatedly rammed the massive stone, wood, and iron door through which I had been shoved. It was to no avail, so I stopped. Softened, diffused sunlight came through the translucent stone of the labyrinth's outer wall, illuminating a gallery parallel to that wall, one with many doors arrayed on both sides of a causeway that led inward. Stretching my legs—joyous action—I limped into that causeway. It widened and became a vaulted chamber, capacious and impressive, with stone seats carved into the sides, niches for torches, and a many-stories-high ceiling that let in a bit of light. On the tiled floor was a heap of twisted metal. This had to be where my father, the white bull, had died. I began to develop an intense distaste for the Vaulted Arena.

Retracing my steps and re-entering the gallery near the entrance, I saw that the gallery's two arms curved in delicate arcs away from the outside door. On the inner part of those crescent arms were a dozen portals, all of them closed and smaller than the causeway that led to the Vaulted Arena. I tried those doors, one by one. A first opened inward to a chamber that was level with the outer gallery and had interior exits leading in several directions. A second's entrance was down a few steps; the chamber itself was small and led to another chamber behind it. A third's entryway was up a few steps, a fourth's led off at a diagonal, a fifth's opened directly onto another door, a sixth's onto an apparently solid wall, and so on. I tried all twelve.

Most of the chambers that I entered from that Entrance Gallery had three doors in addition to the one from the corridor;

some had as many as five. A few had two, and a handful, only one. Clearly, the very differentness of one chamber from another was meant to confuse an intruder or a neophyte not yet familiar with how to get around in the labyrinth. Once beyond those first chambers off the Entrance Gallery, the interior chambers were even more varied in size and arrangement. Two attracted my immediate attention. One was very large and had five doors, and in its center, a deep crevasse—so deep that I could not see the bottom. I named this chamber The Turtle. A second chamber of interest was further to the interior, and it piqued my interest because I entered it several times, each from a different antechamber. It could be entered several ways, but had no exit that led further inward; rather, there was a hatch in its floor. Afraid of what might lie underneath that hatch—although for reasons I could not fathom—I refused to open it. Even so, the room itself was tantalizing, with built-in slabs, shelves holding broken goblets of mica and amulets of obsidian and zephyr, and a sort of preparation bench that was caked with dry powder. In that chamber I also heard water gurgling, but could not locate the source. I called this one the Hollow Cube.

Reinforcing my impression that each and every room was made to deceive was my discovery that no three inner rooms in a row were on the same height level, and that the cumulative direction of the steps was downward. The scarcity of light hampered entry further within; by the fourth level rooms, the gloom inside was indistinguishable from a severely cloudy night. That sent me back to the Entrance Gallery, where I realized that dusk had fallen. No sense trying to explore more, just then, so I propped myself against the translucent exterior wall and tried to sleep.

I remember that night as though it was just a few moments ago—and perhaps, my fellow shades, perhaps it was, for what is time to a labyrinth? A circle? A spiral? A Möbius strip that never ends?

I could not answer that question, but I was acutely aware of other questions that this puzzle of a place had already forced upon me, and a few answers. Who made the maze? Generations of priestesses, and pretty devious ones at that. Had it been altered recently? The evidence was that it had had its exasperation quotient amped up, and by my pal Daedalus. But if human minds had designed the labyrinth, then another human mind—belay that; a *more* than human mind—should be able to figure it out, hmm?

You recent arrivals in Hades Hacienda probably believe that if *you'd* been plopped in that labyrinth, you'd have figured it out. Well, this was not your mother's maze! Not neat, not tidy, not pleasing to the eye like a nice British boxwood hedge-maze. And not like a jagged pattern scythed into a cornfield for the amusement of city-dwellers on vacation. And not even like a slightly more complicated fun house in which the most that happened to you, when you became lost, was that you suffered a bit of a startle and a fright, just enough of a frisson to make you appreciate the more your post-event cocktail.

In your everyday mazes, did you ever feel your stomach drop with the thought that you might very well die in it if you couldn't find a way out?

Bet you didn't. And to be truthful, just then I hadn't yet had that thought either. I still believed there must be a way out of this maze. 'Naïve' was my middle name!

So I tried. While lying in the Entrance Gallery, the next morning, I assembled some hypotheses about potential paths through the labyrinth to an eventual exit. All I needed to do was crack the code! I conceived of each possible path as a tunic to be tried on. After assembling a virtual wardrobe of hypotheses, I set out to don them one by one, to see if they fit the maze well enough to usher me through to an escape point.

Tunic One: The masks are signifiers. There were many terracotta masks, mortared to walls or above doorways, but they were not on every doorway or on every wall. Was there a pattern to the masks? After searching through many inner chambers, I learned that there was no pattern. That tunic didn't fit.

Tunic Two: Gutters. I followed them in the expectation that they might lead to a sewer. Nope.

Tunic Three: Ups and Downs. One set of stairs down, two steps up and out? Maybe. Tunic Four: Dancing Movement. I opted for the door that was a three-quarter turn to the right, and upon reaching the next room I took the exit door from it that was a half-turn to the left. Nope.

Tunic Five: Nomenclature. I only entered rooms that in some way corresponded to the letters of the word 'Goddess,' whose letters I had been taught by Phaedra. Another 'maybe.'

What had I definitively found? Closets, chambers, crannies, cubbyholes, cabinets, cubicles, corners, crevices, and caches—but no obvious exit from the maze.

I returned to a set of rooms that was configured like the layers of an Onion—a set that took me hours to penetrate—where I'd remembered there were ollas infested with grubs and beetles. I found the room and the jars, and downed a handful of insects. They made no dent in my pulsing hunger; rather, by awakening my internal juices they exacerbated it. I had hoped for snakes that fed on insects, but the sacred slitherers whose images graced the walls had vanished—probably taken away by their keeper-priestesses.

A Rogalhida rendered assistance—no, not the deadly scorpion itself but a series of rooms shaped like that arachnid, with recessed arches protruding from a corridor as though they were legs from the belly. To complete the illusion, an upstairs passageway led to a balcony that like a tail doubled back toward the head and beyond it, to end abruptly in an unexpected and deep chasm. Whoa, Asterion, careful there—one more step and its Doomsday!

In the process of returning from the lip of that chasm toward the translucent Entrance Gallery, I again heard the insistent gurgling of water. I'd track it to the source! Took me many hours, but I found it, in another room: a little lion-headed basin into which a cold, clear, bubbling freshwater stream was emptying, as though it came from within the rock.

Water! I lapped it up and thanked the Goddess for it.

Thirst abated, I looked around and saw evidence that many

human beings had traipsed through this Lionhead Basin chamber at one time or another, since the detritus of human habitation was everywhere: amulets on broken cords, ollas of various sizes, candles—I took the candles with me for emergencies—necklaces and earrings of stone and shell, carved-bone connectors for garments, and small stone figurines of the Goddess.

These led me to the conclusion that the cleanup team sent into the labyrinth after the death of Pasiphaë hadn't been very thorough—doubtless an all-male crew who had never been in it before and were likely ignorant of the labyrinth's best treasures. As was I, just then.

I was also thoroughly lost. Trying to find my way back to the main entrance, I went through doors I didn't recognize and smelled scents that contained no hint of my earlier passage. Nuts! I backtracked through an underpass, a connecting defile, and a griffon-decorated chamber until I reached the Onion. From there, I knew the route home.

Traps, conundrums, distortions: what human deviousness!

Animals aren't that deceitful. They don't betray one another. Oh, sure, some animals do dissemble to cheat death or to save their young—but only once in a while. Humans are so frequently, so regularly treacherous that we must conclude that it is a trait of the species. And its not always done to save your life or protect your kiddies. No. Its done by humans for trifles—to get paid, to win a bet, or most often, just for the sheer pleasure of humiliating another human being.

The labyrinth was a monument to human deceitfulness.

Naught to do but learn what it had to teach!

Lesson One: Lust not after sunlight, as the real need is to adjust to the darkness, to train your eyes to more readily pierce the gloom of inner chambers.

Lesson Two: Avoid panicking about the water, to train yourself to venture further from it.

Lesson Three: Whatever direction or portal appears forbidding, therein enter, because the more obviously difficult the passage, the greater the likelihood that it will lead to something of interest.

In other words: comfort and decorum are not your friends. I know that's anathema to you coddled 21ˢᵗ centurions, but there you have it.

What need had I now of human propriety? Of bipedalism? I cast aside my tattered rags and dried bandages, and to fit more easily beneath woman-sized portals I traveled not on two limbs but on four.

On the fifth day, in chambers six or seven levels beyond and below the Translucent Gallery and Vaulted Arena, I found rooms whose furnishings were intact enough to suggest that the rapacious ransackers had never even reached them. These contained heavy powders that dried bare skin at a touch, foul-smelling casks whose contents had long since spilled into the gutters, and bits of old sandals, cracked crustacean shells, and unfinished carvings of stones. I knew not what use I could make of most of these things, but took the chipped stones with me.

On the sixth day, my innards rhythmically throbbing with hunger, I followed a new pattern, gutters in rooms that had no lustral basins, and soon felt dumb for not having earlier figured out that all the troughs emptied not in an exit but toward some coursing water far below. The spillage from the Lionhead Basin trickled down moldy walls until it reached what must be a stream—I could faintly hear it even though I could not see it. Spending time listening to that stream, I figured out that the sound was louder at some times of day than at others. Must be the tide! The labyrinth was possibly above an inlet that led from the sea into the rock walls.

Examining some of the chipped stones, I realized they were flints that I might be able to use, as the servants in the palace did, to produce a spark. In the palace I'd always avoided torches and candelabras, fearful of flames leaping their boundaries and pursuing me, licking at me, clawing at my hair and tail, coming to consume me! Remembering that feeling, I left my hoard of candles unlit.

I hardly needed them, because the ability of my maternal grandsire, Helios, to penetrate the chambers was remarkable.

You 21st centurions don't really know pure dark anymore, because (I have been told) your Middle Realm is so filled with artificial light in every corner and at every hour of the night and day. Ours was not. We had some incredibly dark darks, nights on which the stars and moon were hidden and so when you ventured out of doors you felt as though you were swimming in cuttlefish ink. My eyes were quite large, and I was already somewhat accustomed to piercing the dark with them. In the labyrinth I honed that ability, learning to discern the teeny-tiny increments of light that my grandsire Helios furnished. Really, their ability to penetrate the maze was extraordinary. Soon, with my increased awareness, shadows resolved from murky haze to silhouettes, the cinereous became less obscured, the lackluster warmed to ashen. Talk about your fifty shades of gray! The colors I missed most, in that dark labyrinth, were the primaries, the bright green of the fields, the shocking redness of the poppies, the crystalline blue of the sky.

Where had the Goddess of No Name gone? Had she completely abandoned her temple? If no acolytes worshipped her there, did she even exist?

"Declare your presence, Goddess, if you expect me to worship you!"

That shout felt good; but just in case she didn't like my attitude, I also begged her not to let me inadvertently miss her sign.

On what I marked as the fourteenth day, near crazed with hunger I followed a sequence of griffons around and around until I came to a chamber that stunned me because in it I could hear, far above, the march of guards, the rumbling of wagons, the clanking of metal—it had to be directly beneath the palace! I strained to see toward the top of the chamber, but it was too far above, and in total darkness. The walls seemed to taper upwards, and I figured out that the chamber was a vast, conical-shaped funnel whose shape amplified the sounds from above.

D'oh, you say. Geometry is obvious to you, maybe even second nature, but it wasn't to me, a couple of thousand years before Pythagoras was born on Samos and grew up to codify the shapes used by human beings. All that I could figure out about the Chamber of the Disappearing Ceiling was that if the large end was on its floor, where I was, then the small end, the top of the ceiling, had to be just beneath the palace or actually inside of it.

I shouted upward, "Help me! Help! Me!"

And what did I get in return? You knew it: echoes, nine times louder, mocking my words, sending my pathetic plea back at me.

But my recognition of the funnel's shape then sent me to another chamber, the one I'd entered on the first day, the Turtle. Its central chasm, I now understood, was a yawning circular cone, diminishing in circumference as it disappeared downward. Its shape was the reason why, when I was in it, I had heard the rumble from below—sounds similarly magnified, but in the opposite direction, coming up at me. Those sounds, I now also understood, were not the sounds of human existence—no, not at all: they were the unguent tones of the earth, the creaking and shifting of rock, the low moan of air coursing through cavities, the unmistakable gentle slap of water against rock. The two conical chambers were a matched pair of opposites.

You already had that figured out, hadn't you, my fellow shades? If so, you would also not have been surprised by my next discovery.

Intent on reaching a ninth-level room, at the sixth level my eyes received the impression of a slight increase in light, and my nose and ears, the occasional ruffle of the usually still air. I'd wondered why, in this enclosed space, there had been air currents circulating. With mounting eagerness I followed intensifying light and steadily more volatile air movement. This had to be the escape route! I strained my senses to pursue unhesitatingly the ephemeral rays and tendrils of scent, and, near mid-day, from a ninth-level room I opened a door and rushed outside.

The sun on my upturned face. The wind lightly caressing my hairy, sweated body. The shimmering sky, vibrant and exultant. How wonderful! And yet, and yet—the open area was surrounded by sheer walls, so steep and high that I could never climb them.

The labyrinth's Navel.

My fellow denizens in this dungeon of dungeons, this Hell-hole, this Netherworld: Upon reaching that site I roared in anguish, roared in a way that exceeded all physical pain, roared in heartache, because I now knew absolutely that there was not, and there had never been, and there would never be, any escape route from that labyrinth.

As I stumbled back through the inner chambers, my senses turning in on themselves, I slashed myself with the shard of a broken goblet to see if I could still bleed. I applied rogalhidas to torment my flesh. I defecated on the grinning masks. The mouths of the universe screamed: *Up or down, inside or out, in absolute stillness or in continual movement, none of your actions take you anywhere.*

After a while I calmed—and you know why, my fellow souls. Yes you do. You do, because all of you as adults sooner or later came to the same realization that I had: that there are indeed things about life in the Middle Realm that you'll never be able to change. And you also have realized, as I did, that this knowledge produces a calm—the very certainty of it relieves you of the necessity of constantly trying to alter what cannot be altered, so you can focus more on what you *must* change.

My "aha!" moment led me to very quickly understand that since I no longer needed to spend my days searching for an exit to the labyrinth, I could learn to like the place. After all, it was a temple, magnificently strong and subtle, with infinite layers and resources—I could use it to cultivate the same attributes within myself.

There was so much to explore! Some chambers, munificent in decoration, visually forced a worshipper to his knees. Snake signs abounded, as did those of rogalhidas and dung beetles. On many ceilings, the likenesses of doves fluttered. There were monkeys, hoopoes, peacocks, lions, dolphins.

My inability to decode these myriad images pushed me again close to despair, for how could I be at one with the labyrinth if I didn't really 'get' it? Back in the grazing field, I'd learned how to fit in as a herd animal. In the palace, I'd been instructed in being a sycophant. What did the labyrinth seek to teach me? I did not insist that it reveal all its hidden meanings to me; I was quite willing to accept a depiction of doves as simply a magnet for the eyes, or as significant only for the number of birds shown, or because the doves were not monkeys. But I had a need to discover what it was possible for a novice to learn about the place, if only to take my mind off my hunger.

The days and nights melded into one another. I lost count of how long I'd been Inside. And then I smelled Meat.

Meat! Many times before I'd dreamed of the aroma, anticipated the pounce, the grasp, the thrusting through with horn and tooth, the luscious warmth of fresh blood upon my tongue. Meat! Somewhere in the labyrinth a living human being was present and was stirring delectable pheromes onto the dusty air currents. As I followed the scents toward their source, I learned from them that the being emitting the pheromes was female. She was close to my grasp in the Vaulted Arena, but my approach was too noisy and she successfully fled through one of the doors. Her odors deepened with grace notes of fear and desperation, and I chased those sensations through the concentric rooms of the Onion.

"Asterion? Can we talk?"

The voice that had once caressed me! That chose me as her lover to replace Androgeos, he of blessed memory! That mouth and that vagina that succored me! I brushed aside my amazement at Kharo's presence. Meat! Meat! She didn't really want to talk, else why would she keep moving away from me? Meat! She entered a wholly dark chamber. A few touches on the walls and I knew which one: the Onion's Second Skin. Terrific—she'd be trapped! Meat! She moved haltingly up the steps toward the

Inner Pearl, only to feel at its end the cruel circularity of its small center. I seized her, and to make sure that she didn't topple into the ravine, I deliberately tumbled with her, backwards, down the steps into the gallery. There I bit into her neck with my big front teeth, severing the jugular, releasing geysers of blood and a strangled scream. The blood felt wonderful in my mouth, warm, wet, salty, and slick. How I had longed for its taste! I chomped into her hefty rump, its sweet fat and well-exercised muscles redolent with the jasmine of her last bath. I gulped down big chunks, hardly bothering to chew, and not taking care to prevent her inner juices from unduly slipping down gutters toward the abdominal folds of the earth.

Sated, I dragged her remains into the Translucent Gallery with me and fell into a deep sleep.

Next morning, by the faint influx of light, I took stock. There was no sadness in me at the death of Kharo: I had to eat to remain alive, and had done so. But questions tickled my brain. Certainly, Kharo had been thrust into the labyrinth by Minos. Was this his belated acknowledgment that my journey from innocence to murder had not been my fault? That I'd been seduced, and not only by Kharo? Perhaps. But surely Minos's main purpose in sending her here was to test whether I was hungry enough not to cavil at how my food was presented. Well, the nasty bastard had been correct: I had indeed been hungry enough to eat anything. I hated Minos for being so shrewd.

Breakfasting in a desultory way on Kharo's left calf, I realized I'd made a big mistake: I had killed her too quickly. I should have delayed her death until after we'd had sex.

Fornicate with my victim, slake my sexual need before appeasing my hunger? How awful! How cruel!

How delicious!

A feeling of endless freedom washed over me. Suddenly I had all the time and space in the world. Killing and eating Kharo had been a terrific experience. But I knew now that I could have made it better. Next time, I would! I'd pay more attention to detail. I'd plan my pursuit. A little scare here, a feint there, a false hope presented, a nip—I'd begin with a deliberate bite of a hamstring, to prevent flight …

During my confinement in the labyrinth I had occasionally pondered the question of why I'd been put here. Now the answer had been made manifest: I was here to kill for Minos. I had little choice in doing that, but I resolved not to kill *solely* for Minos. I'd do it for me! To preserve and to perfect myself, so that one day I could kill my tormentor.

You newly-dead souls, you think you'd have reasoned differently? That you would *never* have killed for someone else? That you'd never allow yourself to be trapped in a labyrinth? That you were not a Minotaur but a Minos? Dream on!

Carefully stowing Kharo's remaining parts in a clean, unbroken olla that seemed made for such a purpose, I moved it to the coolest chamber I knew of, and sealed it against rats and bugs. Later, when my hunger again became acute, there would come just the right moment to go to that coldest of chambers, crack open the stored brain pan, and eat the delicacy within. Until that moment, I'd explore my labyrinthine empire and become its master.

Four

Despite my resolve to stay away from the refrigerator, I found myself drifting toward it every day or two, and there nibbling and sucking at Kharo's carcass until there was nothing left but dry bones. Hunger returned. My constant companion, it rendered me subject to visions. Pacing one morning in The Thirteen Portals—as I'd renamed the Translucent Gallery—I saw one through the murky outer wall, a human shape limping by. I halted, and the figure also ceased to move. I limped about, and for a moment the figure beyond the wall repeated and seemed to mock my gimpy progress. Then, though I'd stopped, the figure moved again.

"Daedalus?"

"Yes," came the muffled answer as he moved close to the wall. "Talk slowly."

"Any. Way. Out?"

"There may be. There definitely is a pattern to the rooms. I tried to demonstrate it to you when you were in the cage."

"Your hands on the bars! I'll have to remember. How are things out there?"

"Knossos is an armed camp. A great fleet will sail for Athens to avenge Androgeos. And Ariadne may shortly have some big news."

"What's that?"

"A guard is coming, Asterion. I'd better go."

Daedalus's pattern of his hands on the bars was a melody I tried to play in my head. Oh, my friends, the incompleteness of memory! Was that important day sunny or cloudy? Did your lover say those words, or do you just hope so? Does concentrating on the memory bring it back more fully or serve to flesh out an illusion?

After a day's working on my recall of Daedalus' hands on the bars of my cage, I disinterred five distinct fragments of the pattern. It commenced with a bold, diagonal movement from near the top left corner, down and to the right; followed by a strong, upward, vertical movement to what seemed to be a top edge on the right; then a sweep laterally to the left, past the point where the pattern had begun, all the way to the other horizontal edge; and then down again and to the right on a second diagonal that was parallel to the first.

Beyond those moves, I was fuzzy.

Wait—wait—wait! Where was the start point of the pattern? The entrance portal? Some other wall? Not having enough information on which to decide, I just began moving inward from the Thirteen Portals, and as I trekked through chambers in accordance with the Daedalian pattern a second theme surfaced from my memory, a variant on the first. I worked at that and soon I had five additional lines or slants. Thus far, the pattern never twice traversed the same room—evidence, to me, that I had it correct so far.

Unknowns remained. Where was the starting point? Was the total number of rooms traversed an even number or an odd one? How would I know when I reached the end of the patterns?

Logic dictated that the onset point was the Vaulted Arena rather than Thirteen Portals, since the Arena was where the elders would teach the pattern to novices. Therefore, the mnemonic of the pattern would be … the first letters of the prayer beseeching the Goddess for a bountiful harvest? Nope. Movements through chambers that mimicked those of the Goddess's star in the night sky? Nope again.

An even number of total chambers or or odd number? Surely an odd one. Thirteen? Tried that, but no. Seven, the number of stars in the Goddess's constellation? Uh-uh. Five, the regions of Crete? Naw. Three, the number of steps going into and out of many of the rooms? Mebbe. Nine? Every nine years Minos went to a sacred cave beneath Mount Ida, where Zeus had been nurtured, to consult the leader of all gods. Nine, the sockets in a candelabrum. Nine, the maximum number of steps in a single direction in the labyrinth.

Days and nights on end I played with multiples of three and nine, conjuring line-extensions of the pattern. In daylight I worked in Thirteen Portals and at moonrise transferred my tracing to the dust of the Navel. At length I came to a formulation that fit so well all the known knowns that it *had* to be the answer: A shape of nine times nine, eighty-one. The labyrinth had more than eighty-one chambers, but these nine-squared seemed the most important.

Starting at the Vaulted Arena, I paced the Daedalian patterns through twenty-seven rooms. Thus far, no repeats, no blank walls, and no dead ends, but I was faced with several possible choices of future direction. Through the next hours, by testing and extrapolation I figured out twice twenty-seven more chambers, making a total of eighty-one. By then it was too dark for me to go on. So I returned to Thirteen Portals for the remainder of the night.

Next morning at first light, heart trembling, I moved to the Vaulted Arena and began to traverse the full nine-squared.

Traversing the labyrinth in such a deliberate yet indirect way was not quick work, because there were still lots of decisions to make. Every so often I had to choose whether a particular chamber was or was not part of the pattern, or whether to count such multi-segmented chambers as the Rogalhida as one room or several. I made wrong turns; I retraced my steps; I doubled back. Eventually I arrived at what logic decreed must be the eighty-first unit—that Hollow Cube, not physically far from my starting point, the one with many entrances and the hatch in its floor.

That hatch could not open to nothingness! My journeys in the labyrinth that day had proven that a rational sequence had been built into the maze. Therefore, the hatch exit from the eighty-first chamber had to lead somewhere! To prepare for the possibility of an escape through the hatch, to that Nine-Squared chamber I brought candles and flints, and struck fire and lit the candles in a three-times-three holder. Then, blazing candelabrum in hand, I knelt, opened the hatch, and peered in.

Aagh!

From the darkness below, a hairy, wild-eyed, fierce-toothed, mostly animal face stared at me.

Beneath the hatch was a mirror, the only mirror in the labyrinth.

Once again, as I was on the verge of persuading myself of my humanity, the labyrinth rudely confronted me with evidence to the contrary.

How cruel those maze-makers, constructing their puzzle so that it provided alternate shocks of hope and despair, shearing away a path-seeker's confidence and sanity! Their maze did not merely seek to trap victims, it sought to reduce victims to cowering wrecks, unable to form coherent thoughts.

"Ariadne. Visits. Tonight."

"What, Daedalus? Where? How?"

"Have you found the Funnel?"

"Yes!"

"The mouth is under Pasiphae's bed. I've made a machine. She'll come down in it."

"Why can't I come up?"

"You weigh too much. I must go now, Asterion, or someone will suspect."

"Destroy. The. Cage."

He chortled assent.

In an agony of apprehension, I spent the remainder of the day ferrying to that Chamber of the Disappearing Ceiling candles, flints, unbroken figurines and chalices. Cleansing my matted coat and pungent limbs in the Lionhead Basin, I wrapped my loins in cloth, and struck fire to light candles for Ariadne's arrival.

The rope would break. She would die at my feet. No!—I'd

cushion her fall and we'd crumble together to the floor, there to wake to our passion. I'd impale myself on a sharpened stone and die, become Meat to sustain her until a revolt rescued and enthroned her; for this I'd be posthumously awarded the status of a deity, to whom she would ever after pay homage.

Shortly after sundown I heard the sounds of creaking and grinding, and muffled voices. My nose perked up, as the sounds were accompanied by a sandalwood breeze. Then I could actually see, descending through the darkness, a basket containing the faint outline of a human figure, lit by a single candle. A scarlet-tinted rope, slender as a thread, descended until it touched the floor and snaked in circles. At last, a bell-skirt came into my view, riding in a basket not much larger than a picnic hamper. Then I saw the basket's occupant.

"Phaedra?"

Not Ariadne! Of course not! Ariadne wanted to learn first whether I'd eat the visitor. Disturbed by Ariadne's lack of faith in me, I nonetheless determined to act properly. "Don't worry, little sister, I won't bite you. But did you bring me any treats?"

After a while of continuing to clutch the rope with both hands, after she determined that I wasn't going to attack her, Phaedra kept one hand on the rope and with the other reached her into the folds of her skirt and brought out a honeyed triangle of pastry.

"Baklava! My favorite." I held out my front paw—how cloven it had become!—and allowed her to place the pastry in it. I popped it in my mouth and let the delicious sweetness cool my anger before swallowing it. "How is Icarus?"

"He's going to be my consort when we grow up."

Her golden hair glowed in the torches I had set. I continued to ask questions and to seem happy with her responses until her fingers unclasped the rope and she stepped out of the basket and stood, unencumbered. I walked her around the perimeter, to a figurine. She peered at it.

"Put it in your basket and scurry back up, little one—it's past your bedtime."

She took the figurine with her as stepped back in the basket and tugged three times on the scarlet thread, as casually as though signaling a servant to fetch her chamberpot. A hushed clanking noise then lifted her and the basket smoothly out of the chamber, her image and the single candle's umbra dissolving into the apex until they were fully swallowed by the caliginous dark.

More noise from above. Prepared to confront Ariadne with my anger, I was not ready for the sight of her riding the rope as though it was a favorite horse, her purple- and lilac-tinted bell skirt billowing as she and the basket and candle descended into the torches' glow. Her hair was more lustrous, her facial adornment that of a mature woman.

"You must forgive us for sending Phaedra ahead. Daedalus wanted to be sure that the apparatus would bear any weight."

"The system would have been better tested by lowering a basket stuffed with food, my sister."

"I should've thought of that. You've really decorated the chamber beautifully."

"'If just a few people keep their candles lit, then the city is never completely dark.' Ariadne, I'm going mad. Help me escape."

"I don't know how, Asterion."

"You may know more than you think. Did the priestesses ever talk about being 'below the mirror'?"

"'Below the mirror all is dead.' I remember that."

"Death itself is an obvious exit."

"You speak in riddles, Asterion!"

"I'll be more direct: Get me out of here!"

"Calm down! It's not my fault that you're here! But I'm glad you're caring for the temple, because we priestesses can't guard it from further harm."

"What sort of harm?"

"From falling to pieces. From being demolished by Minos. From being used for unnatural ceremonies."

"Unnatural, you say?"

"Don't taunt me. I must go soon, and there's much to tell you." She emptied her pockets—more pastries, a few raw

50

vegetables. I chewed them gratefully. "Minos lets me keep the snakes and worship the Goddess, but only in private; and in exchange I sit by his side at important state events, and now and then pronounce blessings."

"Over the fleet now sailing toward Athens?"

"We will have satisfaction for the death of Androgeos."

"We will, will we? Satisfaction of what sort? Gold? Tribute? Prayers? When a herd member dies, we mourn and we make sure that they live in our memories, but we don't force anyone else to be miserable."

"Crete has never before feared invasion, and the only reason to fear it now, Minos says, is because our ships are acting so boldly as to make other kings want to strike back at us."

"What does that have to do with me?"

"Everything. Here, take this."

She handed me, from a hidden fold in her garment, next to her bosom, a flat circlet of gold, inscribed with etched lines.

"I treasure it for where it has been lodged, my sister. Ah, it's a labyrinth. Crude, but recognizable. And on the reverse—is that upright bull-creature supposed to be me?"

"Yes."

"I am the symbol of Crete?"

"You and the island are one."

"One the mirror of the other? Then Minos will never allow me out of the labyrinth."

"Don't give up hope, Asterion. I don't despair. Where would we be if we decided to stop pushing for what we both know to be important? Remember, we are the son and daughter of a queen."

I had indeed forgotten that. "You're right, of course. Thank you. I acknowledge that it is dangerous for you to come down here and inform me of all this, and I apologize for doubting you. I will guard the labyrinth."

My first task was not to yield to that terrible mirror in the Hollow Cube. Taking provisions, I descended to the Eighty-

First chamber. The hatch-and-mirror device were meant to conceal. Yet they must be capable of being bypassed. How? Next to the hatch, on a low pedestal was a stone slab whose softly rounded cavity seemed designed to hold a man-sized olla. I pushed against the slab and sensed air swirling near my feet. The mirror was gone! The slab continued to swing easily along the floor until it directly aligned in a position that would allow whatever had been resting in the cavity to be easily tipped into the hatch.

Into the blackened opening I thrust the lit candelabrum. Below the mirror was not nothingness—there was something there!

Stretching away from me, below, was a corridor, spacious enough for two persons to walk abreast. I was tempted to descend immediately, but decided that I must ensure that the hatch stayed open, so I placed a weighted olla on the slab. It fit perfectly and did not move. This led me to believe that the apparatus had been designed to work in just such a fashion, to prevent an accidental closing of the hatch. Then, carrying a candelabrum and with extra candles and flints stuffed into the folds of my garment, I descended through the Mirrorgate.

The light from my candelabrum showed me an awe-inspiring sight, thousands of bones arrayed along the sides of the corridor, human bones so old that they no longer emitted any scent, an uncountable number of them, packed in so tightly that my tugging did not move a single one. Each skeletal part had its niche in this corridor; there were areas of stacked rib cages, of arm bones, of pelvises, of skulls. Further along the corridor, rows of long leg bones alternated with lines of shorter arm bones in patterns of a rectangle, a triangle, a pentagon, a pyramid, a nonagon. These caches were not yet rock-solid, as though they were still being assembled. The entire ossuary design conveyed—what? The fleeting nature of life? The remoteness of the possibility of ever achieving individuality?

Faugh! Metaphor is such a human vice. I prefer logic.

Now the sequence of the upper and lower parts of the

labyrinth became clear. Bodies were disassembled in the upper part and the bones dried, and then afterwards the bones were transported into this corridor and placed below in the appropriate locations. Whose bones? Were all of the dead treated in the same way? At the far end of the ossuary corridor a trail branched off in three directions. Had I come all this way only to discover that beneath the labyrinth lay another labyrinth? Well, I had to explore it. There might be separate rooms for royal bones; for while the ossuary corridor would suffice for ordinary people's bones, royal ones would require better treatment, likely in chambers entered from these several corridors, chambers that themselves might have aboveground entrances to enable living visitors to enter to pay their respects—and through which I might exit!

I raced down the left corridor. Soon the packed dirt-and-stone floor felt wet; as I went on, the footing turned to mud and then gave way to a thin coating of water that deepened as I continued on. There were tiles on the walls and in the walls, and these as well as the stream reflected the gleam of my candelabra.

I halted. Something inside of me grabbed me and held me back. Evidently I feared drowning as much as I feared being burned alive. If this water-filled passageway was the sole route to freedom, I would have to attempt it. But not now. First I would try the other two corridors.

I retraced my steps to the diverging point, and this time took the central corridor. No water. At several points, additional trails branched from it; I stayed on the main, past a downward slope and a reciprocal, gentle incline upward that ended in a solid wall. This must be an important tomb, and it must have an opening large enough to accommodate two priestesses and their burden. I located a device similar to the shifting pedestal at the mirror, a portion of the side wall that bore a handprint you could depress. Despite no longer having a hand the size of a human being, I pressed that area, and the 'solid' wall slid back. From within came the faint scent of the dead. I could not see far into the bulbous cavern without stepping inside. Right near the doorway I spied a rock that was the size and shape of a blackened skull but far heavier. Recalling the need for the weighted urn on the apparatus in the Mirrorgate Chamber, I placed the blackened skull astride the entranceway before entering the cavern.

Inside that cavern my blazing candelabrum revealed a rounded, arched-ceiling space hewn out of stone and earth, and containing hundreds of ollas, arranged in rows. As I moved further into the vast underground storeroom, I heard behind me a rumbling, grating noise. Whirling, I saw the entry port hurtling toward closure. It would latch and I'd be trapped! Then the black skull-stone blocked its way.

Whew.

A weighted trap.

How many such traps did this confounded place have?

More than I could guess, probably.

Several skeletons that were splayed on the floor bore witness that even priestesses could get careless and forget to set the counterweight. I made a quick circuit of the cavern. Each large-mouthed olla held a single adult human skeleton cramped inside, knees-to-chest. Some had fragments of clothing still attached. That meant the bodies had been put into the jars for burial before their flesh had completely decomposed. Most jars were upright; a few had been knocked over, perhaps by earth tremors, perhaps by trapped priestesses. Small openings along the edge of the floor suggested that rats had eaten them.

Having no wish to tarry here, I backed out, pushing aside the heavy sliding door and then replacing the skull-stone in position.

There were not two labyrinths, one above the other; there were two halves of a single entity. In the upper half, priestesses prepared the recently dead, and in the lower half they placed the bones of the dead or the occasional olla containing a VIP. How elegant. How ingenious. How economical.

Acutely aware of being on my last set of candles, I pursued the third corridor. The path changed from cold rock to a hard-packed gravel, and led slightly upward. As I stood at the apex, candles aloft, I heard a rumbling from above, and a panel in the ceiling slid open. Another counterbalance unit, one that must work by means of weight applied below one's feet. I must lift myself off the lever and into the opening—and find a way to prevent the aperture from closing after me when my weight left the lever. There must be a fairly obvious way to do so. I reached up inside the cavity, and my limbs quickly found a heavy stone, seemingly positioned there to be readily accessed. I moved it and placed it on the balance, where it held open the entrance, allowing me to clamber up and through, no mean feat for a bulky being.

A cavernous space, buttressed and divided by vaulting arches. The walls were painted with depictions of the same sort of idealized gardens as the ceremonial rooms of the palace. Perhaps this was the tomb of my mother, Pasiphaë! The thought made my heart leap. There was no queenly bier, however. Even so, I felt a definite emotive tug. In the candles' glow, the painted flowers were magical, the flickering wicks producing the illusion of movement in the figures of animals among the foliage. Along a far wall, in niches, were two catafalques. In a third, niche, a huge standing pithoi, taller than a man, contained amber—and the body of a small boy clad in a purple kilt. Perfectly preserved, his eyes were closed, his mouth slightly open, his arms and legs akimbo as if asleep. This had to be Glaukos, my "sweetly drowned" brother.

The sight affected me powerfully: that helpless child, trapped forever in the solidified honey that stole his breath and life. My cloven hands trembled, my mind spun. I slid down, out of the Children's Garden Cavern, barely halting to replace the counterweight, and raced back toward my part of the labyrinth, the upper half, concentrating only on making sure that the candles lasted. The two small catafalques no doubt held the remnants of other brothers and sisters. I yearned to be with them in their eternal sleep—and yet my body would not let me stay. Hunger forced me to remain alive.

When I re-entered the upper labyrinth, closing the trapdoor beneath me, I no sooner sighed with relief to be on familiar ground than I heard faint sounds and felt slight currents in the usually still air. I hurried to the Descending Cone. The scarlet rope was not in use, yet the noise continued to grow. Human visitors—by the sound, many of them—Meat!—must be in my labyrinth!

Five

An olio of odors, voices, and noises floated into the labyrinth, all telling me that multiple humans awaited me. I salivated to have a satisfying crunch of my jaws on succulent muscle, luscious blood rolling down into my gullet. Yet I feared a concerted onslaught by a substantial host of captives, for their sheer numbers might do me in. Balancing that fear was my certainty that the invaders were merely human, and would have three quintessentially human flaws: an excess of curiosity, a predilection for logic, and heliotropism. Those would be their downfall. The more they searched the maze, the more they tried to reason it through, and the more they sought light, the nearer would they come to being my Meat.

There! A female shrieked in the Receding Cone.

There! A male cursed in the Vaulted Arena.

There! A female sweated when she found herself redelivered into the Gallery of Thirteen Portals.

The startled cries soon yielded to whimpers. The darkness became more hermetic. The odor of fear intensified.

Don't tell me you've never dreamed of killing anyone. You have. Everybody has. While a few of you shades have actually killed other human beings, the rest of you aren't innocent of the thought of doing so. You've plotted murder—yes, you have, I know it! You've dreamed of getting rid of someone who was in your way. Or you've wanted to kill just for the thrill of it. You fantasized about the release it would bring you, the chills up and down your spine; you rationalized that on balance it would be a great experience, one not obtainable in any other way. Of course you then didn't do the dastardly deed—"I had second thoughts." "I lost my nerve." "I forgave my potential victim his trespasses." "The opportunity slipped away."—but you thought about it. Yes, you did! But you didn't do it because you didn't *have* to.

I, on the other horn, had to murder to stay alive. Just as most other animals of the non-vegan sort have to.

So I plotted murder. Every good murder requires a plan. So I sparked fire into wood dust at the base of the tail of the Rogalhida, lit a single candle and left it on the floor. Its glow would enable even a befuddled human to see beyond to the sweep of stairway and precipice, and choose to retreat from that—right towards me! Hunching myself into a recessed doorway of a Rogalhida leg, I settled down to wait.

A white tunic passed me. Female. Wearing sandals. Half-way through the body of the insect she saw the flickering shadows and stopped, transfixed. *D'oh! Dis candle musta been lit by sumbuddy who ain't stoopid or lacking in man-well dex-ter-ah-tee.* On completing her deductive chain, the inhabitant of the white tunic and sandals, rather than coming my way, backed out of the Rogalhida.

I let her go because a larger clutch of potential victims was entering. Two females and a male. They mounted the winding stair, each holding a solid figurine as a club. That was a good choice on their part, but it also let me know that they had not brought with them any more serious weapons. Once they reached beyond the line of the stairs they'd have nowhere to go but over the precipice or into my embrace. I could hardly stop licking my chops.

"There's a sheer drop. We'd better go back."

My cue to enter!

Snorting loudly, I burst from my hiding place and bolted up the stairs. The trio whirled, saw me, and screamed.

No doubt they felt that I was a monster, with my bullish broad face and horns, and my other-than-human torso.

I was jarred too, but by their beauty: two luscious maidens not much older than Ariadne, and a male in first beard.

I snuffed the candle. They shrieked louder. I rushed forward and skewered one female through the ribs even as she bashed my skull with the figurine. Her blow rang in my ears. I withdrew my horn and bit at her wound, savoring the blood as it suffused into my mouth and gave me strength. I positioned my torso to block the stairway so that the other two could not escape.

One to the left of me, one to the right! They charged together—not to battle, as I had expected, but to hurtle past. Tossing my horns, I succeeded in knocking the male backwards. As I did so, the female took the opening to clamber over my rump at the inner wall and bound down the stairs.

I let her go too, content with the food in my jaws and the all-but-immobilized male on the precipice. Chewing through the creamy fat, spitting away gristle, cracking bones with delight, I found a certain unexpected sweetness to the Meat. So fresh! So young! So tender!

I had imagined the best parts to be the muscles of the inner thigh, especially in people used to riding horses. They did not disappoint. I avoided piercing the bowel with its foul contents, a mistake I had made with Kharo.

From the precipice a scream scored the air, steadily diminishing in volume until it was replaced by the thump of a body hitting rock, then a last faint groan.

A suicide. Now that Meat was gone.

But I chewed on the Meat in my jaws, and hoped that my hunger would now abate. It didn't. This victim just sort of whetted my appetite, and not only for food—for killing itself, and for the associated pleasures of tormenting my victims and being the dominant lord of this labyrinthine universe.

Did such an insatiable craving prove that I really was a monster? To show that I was no monster I abandoned what remained of the female's body, uneaten, on the landing of the Rogalhida's Tail, where it could serve as a warning to the other potential victims not to approach the precipice.

I moved quietly toward the Gallery of Thirteen Portals, so that my emergence would surprise whoever was in it. I startled four exhausted young men and women, one pair with arms entangled for warmth, and two singles, a male and a female, each propped individually against the translucent wall. All squealed and scrambled for four different doorways in what seemed to be a planned maneuver. As they did, a roar came—not from these captives but from the opposite direction, from behind me, from beyond the translucent wall of the labyrinth, from a horde of watchers!

"It's the Minotaur!"

"He's awake!"

"There he is!"

"Kill, kill, kill the Athenians!"

"Go get 'em, Asterion!"

Who were these Cretans? What sort of human beings would cheer on my killings? What ghouls these mortals be!

I had no time for this exhortatory crap. There was prey to catch. Turning away from the translucent wall, I reached for an interior portal.

As chases go, it was a rather good one. Lasted for hours. Full of decoy, gambit, plateaus of waiting, and the slow removal of options from the target. Ignoring clues that might have led me to the others' hiding places, at last I forced a young lady to enter the Cruelest Chamber, a cube with four doors, three of them leading to blank, impassable walls. Daedalus had outdone himself with this space. I found the young lady there, pressed against one of the false exits, unable to accept that it would continue to deceive her: she was a white-garbed beauty, long-limbed, fair of face, and suffused with dread.

Perfect!

And she could see me. I slowly unfastened the cloth about my loins. At the undraping, her whimper became more aggravated.

"No, no, please don't do this! Stop! Stop! Apollo, save me from the beast!"

"Apollo will not help you here, my lady."

While she was taken aback by hearing me speak, and in her own language too, I stripped away her tunic, revealing in the gloom a body on the verge of lushness. Taking advantage of my momentary infatuation, she slashed at my left eye with a splintered chalice, missing the orb but scoring my forehead, causing blood to drip into my eye and blur my vision.

I butted her hand away. She attacked again, drawing blood from my forearm. Did she not understand that all I was looking for was a good time?

I rammed her against the wall. She slid down, blood pulsing from her mouth and from where bones poked through the soft flesh of her torso. Her eyes assumed a querulous, childish look that slowly congealed into an inflexible stare.

"You have the effrontery to die?"

I destroyed her then, tossing her on my horns and stomping until her eyes could not stare at me. Then I ran from this mass of flesh that was no longer worthwhile for sexual purposes, galloping through corridors and galleries.

"You Athenians—I'll get you! You killed my brother, and now you're forcing me to be a monster!"

Finding none of them, on a jog around the Gallery of Thirteen Portals I butted the translucent wall, an action greeted with cheers by the crowd assembled outside. To flee the crowd I limped through dozens of chambers until I reached the Navel— only to find more watchers gathered far above, at the edges of the surrounding cliffs. They not only saluted my appearance, they showered me with bouquets of flowers and with those coins of the labyrinth and its monster.

Insult added to injury! Ducking back inside, after careening from chamber to chamber I reached a central room with three lustral basins, and there discovered two young men. They attacked me with fervor, and for a while the three of us had a nice tussle, but they were ultimately no match for me. I killed them both. Tearing a rack of ribs from the nearest boy, I chewed on it to calm down.

My plan for an orderly series of killings had been ruined. One visitor had escaped me by suicide; another's half-eaten torso now

61

lay in the Rogalhida Tail; she who had refused my attentions was all pulpy in the Cruelest Chamber; and here before me were two deader-than-doornail males. The messiness of all this was disconcerting.

I had let rage get the better of me. Equally unsettling was that my rage had been tonic to those Cretans watching me through the translucent panels of the Entrance Gallery and from the cliffs above the Navel. The more I resembled the beast depicted on their coins, the more they liked it.

Nothing worse than being forced to inhabit your caricature, is there?

I refused to perform further for them. I fled down several levels, to a chamber that the crowd outside could not see and that the remaining visitors to the labyrinth were unlikely to stumble across, the center of the Turtle, the Cone Descendant, that large, circular space with the deep, descending vortex, the funnel that served as a megaphone multiplying the sounds of the great forces below.

Think, Asterion, think! What to do? How to live? What to eat, other than human flesh? At such moments, I wished that I had no human-ness at all, that I could just exist as an animal does, without having to reflect on the appropriateness of one's own activities to obtain food to sustain life. Oh, my fellow souls in Hades Domain, an animal just is; it doesn't have to think so much about the act of existing. It just is. But try as I might, I couldn't shake the human side of me.

Mulling over the awfulness of my half animal, half-human existence, after a while I began to hear and feel the rhythmic breathing of the tide far below, the murmurs of vast masses of rock as they minutely shifted their bearings. The voices of the earth were distinct and discordant, until after a while further they began to mesh and to coalesce into a single, deep, harmonic voice.

"I am he who sent the bull to your mother," that voice said to me. "I am he who sends the captives to you. I am he who rules the seas and the inner earth. How fragile, how temporary is this island that Minos thinks he commands. I, your true father, I toss him about—toss you about!—toss the earth and seas about!—for reasons that are mine alone to know!"

The voice thrilled me and shocked me. Was I truly Poseidon's son? I had so many questions for him!

"Minotaur! Oh, Minotaur!"

A voice—not from the depths, not male, and not from a god. It belonged to a female Athenian. I laughed at that voice, because after hearing Poseidon speak to me I now knew that wherever in the maze this distaff Athenian was, she would have to submit to a force as irresistible as the sea.

Dusk smothered the labyrinth as I pursued her scent and sounds to an antechamber of reclining benches that was nearby to the Vaulted Arena, whose ceiling let in more light than elsewhere in my labyrinth. A roseate glow suffused the walls and revealed the young woman resting there. Dark-haired, bright-blue-eyed, slender and rather short, this was the one who had twice evaded my grasp, the first time by gathering comrades to accompany her to the Rogalhida's Tail, the second by deflecting my attention to the male on the stairs so that she could escape.

"I know what you want," she whispered as she caught sight of me. Then, lowering herself into a supine position, she unfastened her tunic and pleaded, "Don't hurt me."

My mind being set on rape, I was unprepared for welcome; but I coped. Afterwards Nereida, who had been a virgin, claimed pleasure in our joining, and I had seen no evidence to the contrary. The urge to destroy still plagued me, but just then I held it back. There would be time enough for carnage.

"How many of you are there? I mean, *were* there?"

"Seven boys, seven girls. Is there really no way out?"

"I've found none, but you are welcome to scrutinize every prospect and if you locate an exit to take it, alone, or with your friends, or with me. Until then, we are all trapped in the labyrinth. And I'll eventually have to kill you all."

Nereida fastened her outsized blue eyes upon mine and said, "I'll help you with the others if you'll promise not to eat me."

This proposition struck me as nothing else had in my moments in the labyrinth; I rolled on my back and laughed and laughed until I could laugh no more. By the time I had recovered my composure, Nereida had vanished from the chamber. Resisting the impulse to track her, I lit a few candles and awaited developments.

Shortly she returned in company of two other women—both attractive, disheveled, and frightened. Xentha was tall, vulpine and wiry; Oikolos was stockier, with ample teats. They too displayed the wide-eyed, grim restlessness and frantic terror born of their situation. Since they had anticipated instantaneous death upon being thrust into the beast's lair, they were unprepared for what was happening now. Their personalities had begun to shatter on the obsidian anvil of the labyrinth. Very quickly they agreed to sex with me, separately or in any combination.

Ah, my friends in Hades' Hostel, one of the few pluses of being in Netherworld is no longer needing to dissemble about our past sexual experiences. No bragging, no fibbing, no glossing over of inadequacies. A relief, isn't it? And so I tell you, frankly, that my initial bouts with the three maidens were decidedly mediocre. Virgins, they were so terrified and unpracticed that pleasure was only fitfully evident and was certainly not happily contagious.

My attempts to be gentle and kind seemed to them obviously false, not a stimulant. I tried entertaining them, juggling several small ollas, but their amusement did not translate into passion. I resisted the urge to smack them around but, annoyed, at last I began to issue orders: You stroke this, you lick that, you do this to her and I'll do that to you.

Worked like an amulet!

After my instructions, they did as bidden and soon rewarded me—and themselves—with little enthralled moans, beads of sweat, and bouts of inspired innovation. Once loosened up, they had a heck of a time.

You don't believe me? You say that the idea that the victim wants it and enjoys it is naught but the boast of a rapist? Well, I grant that I had dreams of conquest, but at that moment force was not the main issue with these women. How do I know? Because when the first bout of coupling was over, one of the young men came out of hiding and joined us, quickly reaching for Xentha. The heat of that pair's carnality convinced me that they had been longing for one another for some time. Now I recognized them: the lanky pair with close-cropped hair, part of the quartet I had surprised in the Gallery of Thirteen Portals. Cheon was his name, and when he realized I enjoyed watching him with Xentha, he suggested that we all decamp to a more capacious spot and have at it.

In the Vaulted Arena we lit candles and had sex with one another, in various combinations. The recently-deflowered became indefatigable. Their intensity was heightened by knowing there was no tomorrow, and that whatever they did here would surely stay here. The candles gradually went out, and in darkness we continued grappling, suckling, pushing, caressing, tickling, slapping, penetrating, and nibbling without much regard for who was doing what to whom.

When morning came I was wary, thinking that now they might join together and attack me, but their exhaustion, coupled with their sexual satiation, had stilled their aggressiveness. A few additional white-clad Athenians came out of hiding places, wanting their share of the festivities, and permuting the possibilities of combination and celebration. I plunged in again and had to be careful in my passionate nips, but so must we all at times, don't you agree? The tide of Poseidon ran strong in me, and through me to bless and energize my comrades.

During the darkest hours of the next night, with the air about me punctuated by the snores of the Athenians, I conceived a wonderful plan. Minos had sent these virgins to the labyrinth to be killed and eaten. To thwart him, and to maintain my sanity—and sustain my pleasure—I would keep as many of them alive as I could, and for as long a time as possible. Toward morning I awakened Nereida and told her to assemble everyone in the Vaulted Arena. Her blue eyes gleamed with triumph, as though I had acceded to her wish to let her be in charge of the others and remain safe from my horns.

I toured those locations where half-eaten bodies lay. The odor emanating from the dead female in the Cruelest Chamber was discernible a half-dozen levels away. Approaching that other room where three of the four portals led to blank walls and the dead males lay, I could also sense the nearby presence of living flesh, but I ignored it to concentrate on my task of cleaning and storing the Meat.

And then the captives shoved the stone door shut behind me.

Trapped! I had underestimated their ingenuity!

The closed portal was virtually immovable. Beyond it I heard male voices telling one another to pile up pithoi and stones to buttress the barrier. After a while the scrambling noises and human sounds faded away. I knocked my horns against each of the walls, to compare their echoes. The blank doors were impassable, but between the second and third there was a hollow sound. With some difficulty I wrenched from the chamber floor the single lustral basin, and with it lodged against my forehead and extending forward of my horns, I flung myself at the hollow-sounding area. The basin and I crashed through into another chamber. My head rang with pain but I was free again.

And enraged.

I'd kill them all! And enjoy it! Why were they so stupid as to refuse to recognize that I was their only possible redeemer? They'd pay for their effrontery!

My amateur trappers had made no contingency plans for my escape. They scattered. I tracked their scatter route. Easy! Used to the labyrinth, I could plan three and four moves ahead. They took wrong turns and had to double back; I knew my path. They ran; I walked. They made noise while trying to be silent; I sang a song that sprang into my head:

Lord of the waters
We tremble at thy sign,
Accept our wet offerings:
Blood, honey, and wine.

At this threnody, two panicked males emerged from their hiding places into a corridor with three doors. I charged the central door, forcing my prey to flee through the side exits. Having split the captives, I followed the one who took the left door, whose flight pattern was to always to make left turns and to choose steps leading up rather than down. I bent this left-footed light-seeker toward the Vaulted Arena, and caught him in an olla-filled antechamber on its fringe.

My fellow shades, since I reached Hades' Holding-pen, I've interviewed many serial killers, and have learned from them that for the most part they preferred finishing off their victims in secret, unseen and unheard. Cowards! I had always imagined that my dispatching of the sacrifices—my future murders—were not only for me to savor, they were for others to witness and to be inspired to fear. While I was still constructing that theory, this first batch of sacrifices provided me with an opportunity to prove the point. Having trapped one Athenian male in an olla-filled chamber, I put the theory to the test by not killing him then and there, just seriously disabling him—because I needed him to scream loud enough for the others to hear. Only after his ability to scream had been exhausted did I crush him against a wall, stuff his carcass into a wide-mouthed olla, hoist the jar onto the resting place of my horns and forehead, and with it as a crown, enter the Vaulted Arena.

Near the center of the room, illumined by a thin shaft of sunlight, was the twisted heap of metal on which my father the white bull had once perished. Six youths and maidens in tattered white tunics lay and sat in various places in the chamber.

With their dozen human eyes fastened upon me, I smashed the olla carried on my horns down onto the jagged metal rack; the pottery burst into a hundred fragments and revealed the bloodied, distorted body within.

"You can die this way," I roared at my wide-eyed visitors, "or we can party on!"

Looking back on that dramatic moment, I can brag that my point was well made. No doubt it was Poseidon's moment, manifested in actions that only seemed to me to be of my own volition. Yet it pleased me and, I must add, it sure did soften up my audience. Thereafter they would hear, really hear, the essential message I needed to convey to them: "We are imprisoned here together, in all likelihood until death. Every one of us will end our days in the Middle Realm here, including me—but there's no need for us all to die soon! We have a source of water and a source of food. I've eaten portions of your comrades, but having done so I'm no longer as famished. That is why I can make you this one-time offer: Meat, freshly killed. Sustenance and strength. Eat of it and live."

"Never," said one youth. Was it he who took the right turn and thereby escaped me?

"Don't be finicky. So long as you are alive, there's always hope. Cannibalism is preferable to starvation. Commit the act and atone for it later."

"The gods forbid it," whispered the most statuesque woman.

"Take it up with them when you cross the Styx."

At that moment the gods seemed very far away, while here and now, hunger gnawed at the captives.

"How can you speak calmly of such matters?" cried Oikolos, who displayed a fine supply of Meat.

"Don't you see that by offering to share my food, I am whittling down the time that I can remain alive?"

"No, you're merely preserving your food intact rather than letting it decay," Nereida stated. "What is the price for our cooperation? What do you want from us?"

"Companionship. Entertainment. And above all, information: I want you to tell me everything that you know about the world."

Here was gabbro, a hard rock; there was softer chlorite, more likely to have been bored through to make the labyrinth's many rooms, and yonder was serpentine, whose veined patterns might be followed to possibly yield further clues to the labyrinth's design. Some women liked to be touched lightly, others roughly. A walk in the sunlight without cares and with the right companion was as good as sex. One Minotaur-embossed coin would buy an ox-cart's burden of wheat. The road from Piraeus to Athens was similar to but steeper than the road from Amnisos to Knossos. Little brothers were always pests. Mothers who spared the rod and spoiled the children were loved by their offspring no more and no less than were strict disciplinarian mothers. Plural nouns required singular verbs. Raw fish could give you diarrhea. Suspicion was frequently leveled against pubescent boys who took too many baths.

I also learned that the song that sprang from my lips during the chase was familiar to them—it had been a favorite of the young woman that I killed on the stairs of the Scorpion. Wow! There was something to the old priestesses' tale that one acquired another's knowledge by ingestion!

To give my companions less reason to quibble, I removed the heads of the dead victims and separated the limbs and the parts of the torsos so that the pieces would remind them less of individuals. The coldest chamber I'd found was one that had Three Basins. It became our Meat-storage locker. I tried to persuade the more recalcitrant Athenians—those who believed that eating flesh would doom them to a harsh and awful afterlife—that the gods erected similar taboos for every aspect of human life, so that no matter how carefully mortals tried to live they were likely to break one or another of the rules.

We stone killers are great rationalizers.

I also had on my side time and the universal urge to remain

alive. On the first occasions on which my visitors ate of their dead companions, they returned from Three Basins with stricken looks on their faces. But by the third sessions they were merely burping. A half-moon after my display in the Vaulted Arena, they had set in place a complex set of rules for dining. Anyone could go to and eat a portion of Meat; candles and flints were cached for those who preferred to have a roast; taking a companion to lunch was permitted; refusal to accept an invitation was not stigmatized, nor was insistence upon dining alone.

"No, thank you; I'm not hungry today," Iola would say to every invitation. Bony to begin with, she became even more so and was the only one of the survivors to completely abstain from food. A starvation artist! As she thinned, her conversation dulled, and she participated less and less in our sexual joinings. I ought to have killed her to prevent the loss of her flesh, but even I could not bear to snuff her fading candle. She lingered on, an ethereal reproach. We also admired the pledged lovers Xentha and Cheon, both lanky, with coal-dark hair, black-irised eyes and prominent long noses. "When we sleep, Asterion, neither of us has dreams." Believing that they would never leave the labyrinth alive, they ate, copulated, bathed, explored, and conversed with smoldering intensity.

"Life doesn't really belong to us," Oikolos said to me during a post-coital conversation. "Life is a tunic borrowed from a queen, for use only on this special occasion, and must soon be returned." The chunky one never wanted to eat alone and always wanted sex for dessert. I spoiled her.

My delight in Oikolos annoyed Nereida, who still hoped that her baby blues made me her eternal slave. I told Nereida that vanity had already proved her downfall.

"How so, Asterion?"

"You entered the beauty contest, didn't you?"

Aegeus, rather than scour the countryside and abduct people for the sacrifice, had sponsored a contest that brought willingly to his collection point the loveliest of lissome lasses.

Top prize in the contest had been won by Murex, a facially

exquisite and perfectly proportioned young woman who even in the labyrinth liked to stride about, striking statuesque poses. Back on the mainland, the desires of Ptach and Tsingas to copulate with Murex had led to their easy capture. In the labyrinth, though, after the boys' initial bouts of sex with Murex they did not seek repeat encounters. I wondered why. It was that while Murex always expected to be adored, during copulation she did no more than smile benevolently at her partner's efforts.

We labrynthians achieved a state of such near continuous arousal as to distract us from our insistent hunger. We thought we were being excitingly decadent, although later I would understand that with this first set of captives I had only grazed the surface of pan-sexuality and had not even begun in bondage, sado-masochism, the drinking of blood, and other excitation games.

My partners had satisfactory numbers of orgasms, and I was quite regularly induced to my own eruptive ecstasy by mouths, vaginas, anuses, hands, and sometimes just a lot of back scratching. But it wasn't enough. Immersed in lust, I yearned for that carefree walk in the sunlight with the right companion.

My cohabitants' lectures to me on Athenian, Spartan, and other Peloponnesian history, on animal husbandry, on mathematical possibilities, all receded in interest because we were sending each other sexual signals in class. Nereida's wish to control, so obvious in her tutorial on agricultural economics, ran afoul of the iron of Oikolos's childlike refusal to see things the teacher's way. The two women stopped speaking. In the moral hegemony seminar, Ptach argued that exclusivity was wasteful, and cast aspersions on our bonded pair, Cheon and Xentha. Others whispered that Ptach thought he was more entitled to Xentha because Cheon was of lower social status. The young male rivals exchanged harsh words, then angry and insolent stares. Xentha, with tears of entreaty, vowed fealty to Cheon but for harmony's sake left the door open to a quickie with Ptach. One day Xentha and Cheon went to Three Basins for a meal, and Ptach followed; believing they were taking too long, and likely to be also having sex, Ptach burst in. Outraged at the interruption, they slew Ptach with a thighbone.

This kill of theirs did not make me feel cheated. We added the dead Ptach to our diminishing cache of flesh. Iola followed him into death, although by then there was little of her to nibble. In the cache, bones and Meat intermingled until we did not know who had been whom, a confusion that comforted my companions.

Most of them had now come around to the position of understanding that the strictures on sexual liaisons, touted to them in the outside world as of great importance, were not, they were the invention of prudish humans. Therefore, those barriers could now be tossed away. However, the captives continued to worry about the gods' sanctions against murdering other humans.

"Self-defense is a usual and reasonable justification for murder," I told them, based on my having sat at Minos's feet during his cases, and citing Cheon and Xentha's slaying of Ptach. "Extreme hunger is another. My belief is that the gods measure us not really on whether we have sinned, but in relation to how well or how badly we have accomplished the tasks that the world presents to us. And in this labyrinth, my friends, our task is simple: We must choose between cannibalism and suicide. For all we know, in the gods' eyes the latter may be worse."

"You justify sin more artfully than the most corrupt priestess," Nereida said as we washed up in the Lionhead Basin. "You soothe the consciences of the guilty because you are the most blameworthy among us."

"And you are the most decent?"

"I have already been certified as a sacrifice to the gods."

"What human or god can judge me—judge you—judge any of us for what we do here? Are we to measure our actions against standards of behavior reachable only by those too holy to have truly lived on this earth?"

"The longer you survive, the heavier your burden."

"There's no way to stop either your onus or mine from growing, Nereida, so for a while let us defy the gods by giving to each other great pleasure."

She laughed, grabbed my head in her hands, and urged my mouth toward her spreading legs. What ensued was a coupling so fervid that my every pore throbbed with its thrill. Nereida's orgasms brought her to tears.

In the aftermath, we sat listening to the gentle murmur of the water in the basin.

"Will you do something for me, Blue-Eyes?"

"Anything," she vowed.

"Stay alive!"

The fragrances of crocus, lily, and anemone assailed me as I roamed the corridors one day, and they grew stronger as I neared the Receding Cone. On the floor of that chamber were three bouquets, their stems split, blooms curling, colors fading. Clutching them to my nostrils, I reproached myself for neglecting to make regular visits here. My human companions' senses of smell were limited, so they had not discovered the flowers, which was fortunate for they would have asked their origin. One bouquet was almost dust, the second had shriveled, the third was flaccid but nearly whole. None had been crushed, as would have happened had they been dropped from that considerable height, so they had to have been placed here by someone after a descent to the floor, the last bouquet very recently. I lit a candle as my own signal, and lay beside it. Try as I could to calm myself for a new encounter with Ariadne, I was apprehensive, fearing another trick. From further within the labyrinth I heard the Athenians faintly calling my name, but did not respond. Shortly, the scarlet rope began to descend with its basket, which seemed larger. The delicate sandals, the well-turned ankles, the belled skirt, the faint perfume of vaginal warmth: It was indeed Ariadne. The regal robes mirrored the purple, orange and white of the floral harbingers. Her scent told me that she was no longer a virgin. The thought enraged me against her unknown conqueror and suffused me with an intense need to carnally possess her myself.

"What's taking you so long to dispatch them?," Ariadne said

as she alit. "This is my fourth visit since they were sent in. We are quite upset about this."

"'We?'"

"Myself. Daedalus. Phaedra. Icarus. And Minos, of course."

"The king knows that you descend into the labyrinth?"

"No, Minos does not know that I come down here, Asterion. But he *does* know about the sacrifices. Who d'you think sent them?"

"I have long since determined that, my sister. Fourteen lives for Androgeos's—unequal redress, wouldn't you say?"

"A blood tax, Asterion. Part of a grand design that will make us the commanding power of the Cycladean seas."

"'Us?'"

"The royal house of Crete," she said, enunciating each word. "Just do what you're supposed to do, and I promise that you'll never be hungry again, and that your countrymen will honor you forever."

"Will you?"

"I remain your devoted adherent. I immensely admire your fortitude, patience, and capacity." She stepped closer, as though to demonstrate that she trusted me still. "Our only hope, Asterion, is to join Minos for the moment, to make him feel that he commands our fealty—until the day that we overthrow his empire from within."

"You and I together, as we dreamed in the past? Just rise up and do it?"

"Yes!"

"I have given up puerile dreams, Ariadne, just as you have given up being a little girl. Is Minos your lover?"

"No!" she shouted, clutching her abdomen as though stabbed. "How can you say such an awful thing?"

I was about to detail the olfactory and psychological evidence for it when I heard shuffling noises from the direction of a nearby corridor.

"Asterion! As-steer-ee-on!"

Moments later, Oikolos entered the conical chamber. Spotting me, the fleshy girl broke into a smile as though she had just triumphed at hide and seek; then, upon seeing Ariadne in her royal skirt, Oikolos's jaw dropped. Next, upon realizing that the basket and scarlet rope were an exit out of the maze, she reverently whispered, "Thank the gods," grabbed the rope, and started pulling herself up, hand over hand. Beneath those fleshy arms were biceps of iron.

Ariadne threw herself at Oikolos to knock her off the rope and basket. The two women fell to the floor and tangled, each trying to seize the basket while seeking to prevent the other from doing so. The apparatus began to ascend—Daedalus must have interpreted the tugging as the signal for rescue. With a leap, Ariadne broke free of the desperate Oikolos, jumped up to grasp the red line, and let it pull her out of range even before she stepped wholly into the basket.

"Kill her!" Ariadne shouted.

Oikolos shrieked, stared at me and hastily fled the room.

"Why should I kill her, Ariadne? How would that make things better for me?"

"Idiot! She'll tell the others that I was here ... ruin ... everything!" Ariadne's voice steadily diminished in volume as she disappeared inside the cone.

"Maybe I will kill her—if you tell me who your lover is," I shouted after her rapidly receding skirt.

"Dae-da-lus!"

How obtuse of me not to have deduced that! But just then, were I to stop to unravel its implications Oikolos might indeed reach the others, spread word of the scarlet rope—and produce chaos. All that I had accomplished in winning the captives to my side would vanish, instanter, and I'd have to battle them all together. I set out to find and kill Oikolos before she could convey what she had seen.

Cruel, you say? Unnecessary, you shout? Oh, that Minotaur, blinded by Ariadne! Once ordered to do her bidding, he too willingly abandons reason and morality.

75

True, I suppose; but not the whole truth.

Ah, my fellow sufferers in Hades' Domain, I was not eager to kill Oikolos of the wonderfully yielding embrace, Oikolos who never wanted to eat alone. But Ariadne was correct: Oikolos could not be permitted to blab. I resolved to limit the chubby one's suffering. Other victims I had noisily tracked through the labyrinth; Oikolos I pursued in crafty silence, and was able to come upon her from the rear, unobserved, in Poseidon's Chamber. The lovely haunches had lost their dimples! Perhaps I could allow her to remain alive if she would agree not to say anything to the others about the scarlet rope. She whirled, saw me, and trembled.

"You promised you'd never hurt me, Asterion."

"And I don't want to hurt you now." I reached for her.

"Don't touch me," she shuddered, and stepped back.

Was it deliberate or just a slip? Oikolos slid down the conical floor of Poseidon's Chamber and disappeared among the rocks and the murmuring stream far below.

Black mists of tears swirling before my eyes. I prayed for my fleshy love: "Poseidon, great god of the waters, convey this child of the earth to your sea, and make of her one of your dolphins, so she may exclaim your beauty and power by her leaps into the sunlight."

Ariadne had hurt me in three ways: by siding with Minos even as she professed continuing adherence to revolt; by taking Daedalus as her lover; and by inciting me to kill Oikolos.

In the Vaulted Arena I told my companions of Oikolos's accident and my sorrow at it, but I could sense that some did not believe I hadn't caused her death. Perhaps to assure them that I spoke honestly, I let them in on a big secret: "There is an inner labyrinth, and it may contain an escape route."

"What?" "Where?"

"It devolves from the Eighty-First Chamber—ossuary passageways that lead to a series of royal tombs in which Minos's relatives are buried. Those tombs may contain passageways to the Outside."

"Let's go!"

Six

Through the Mirrorgate of the ninth-squared chamber I soon ushered the five remaining Athenians, the females Nereida, Murex, and Xentha, and the males Cheon and Tingas. The possibility of escape was a fog beautifying an otherwise harsh landscape. The visitors gasped at the ossuary corridor with its walls of arranged bones. "Think of order and artistry," I urged. "Here is the hand of woman tidying the chaos of nature, superseding the randomness of death." We pushed on and entered the Childrens' Garden Cavern. At the doorway I demonstrated how to recognize and neutralize the trap, and then held the counterweight so they could safely enter and exit my siblings' resting place.

"This trap certainly would have caught me," Cheon opined, on the way out. "Most people would hesitate to touch that blackened skull." Last to exit from the catafalques' garden was the exquisite Murex, who continued to gaze at the colorfully painted walls with their gay nursery scenes.

"You have now penetrated as far as I have ever gone into this lower maze. Further progress is as much up to you as to me."

"Consider this," Cheon argued to us: "Since we are near the north coast, the best chance of a path leading to a sea channel exit is the northern route."

"Consider this," Nereida responded: "The priestesses in charge of obsequies thought not of escape but of burying important personages near where their relatives might be able to visit. That's why we should search for the most recently constructed tombs, which could have openings to the outside."

The other captives were silent: Even when their lives were at stake they wouldn't offer an opinion. What followers! I suggested we try Nereida's suggestion first, and we set off on a hunt that elated me because it was that of a herd with a single, shared purpose, and because I'd have company to steady my nerves when we got to the point where the flowing stream had previously halted me.

To make up for our having chosen Nereida's idea rather than Cheon's, he seized the lead, and thus was the first of us to encounter the water, initially as muddy footing, then as a cool stream that deepened, slurring our walking rhythm and producing startlingly loud echoes in the cramped corridor. Lagging deliberately, I could see the water level rise on Cheon: ankle-high, knee-high, testicle-high, waist-high, chest-high. My heart pounded. The Athenians were not discomfited; several pulled their hands through it in swimming motions. I tried not to panic. Our candle flames leaned to the right. "An aqueduct," Cheon announced, sweeping his hand from left to right. "Blocked," he concluded after looking. He strode on ahead and we followed.

As he sloshed on, the water level on his body receded. Reaching the central spot where he had paused, I felt tile beneath my feet and saw tile on the walls of the passageway that was at right angles to ours. Cheon was correct: this was an aqueduct. Beyond the reach of the candles I spied the faint outline of metal bars whose pattern was distinctly Daedalian. This stream might be the water source for the palace, one that ran underneath the walls and emptied into a cistern. A possible escape route? I didn't take it, as I was afraid I'd have to submerge my head and risk drowning to go in the direction of an uncertain destination. I tried to calm myself, slogging on until my toes grasped the familiar, cold, hard, passageway floor.

Three additional branches presented themselves, none of which was the obvious continuation of the main trunk. Cheon opted for a right turn. Fifty paces further on, beyond what we had been able to see from the choice point, the branch came to an abrupt dead end.

"Let's retrace our steps, Asterion."

"Not yet. This may be the route to other royal burials. There could be a tomb behind this wall."

"And a trap?"

"I see no trap—but the wall itself is soft. Chlorite. This space may not have been completely prepared before Minos closed up the labyrinth." I began tearing at the relatively soft chlorite of the wall. My hands had become distressingly cloven and proved too clumsy, and so, changing tactics, I used my horns to chip away at the barrier. Several emboldened Athenians used their fingers to pry out some of the bones and skulls embedded in the wall; the fragments of bone then made for additional digging implements. Many candles and much effort were expended until Nereida called for us to halt, because she had heard a hollow sound.

"I'll punch it through."

I did, and a sour stench emerged and grabbed at our throats: decaying flesh. Indeed, this must be a recent tomb. Behind the hole was a solid mass. Jointly, Cheon, Tingas and I managed to reach in and topple the blockage with a resounding crash whose reverberations hinted at a cavernous internal space beyond.

"Nereida, you're the smallest. Go ahead in. Here's a candle."

Holding it before her as a talisman to ward off evil, she clambered in and moments later came out again. "This is the tomb of Androgeos," she announced with a grim face. "Go in, if you like; I'll wait here."

"How do you know it's his?"

"The laurels."

Her cryptic bitterness was unexpected. I butted one horn in earnest against the chlorite at the side of the hole, crumbling it to accommodate my withers. Once inside, we had to step over the toppled stone monument. It lay in two pieces on the floor, the carved athletic wreath, and its bulky pedestal. Candles revealed that, like the palace, this space was spare and whitewashed. In the position of honor was a sarcophagus with Androgeos' name and royal rank carved into its cover, according to what the

Athenians told me. Also in the chamber, near the sloping walls of the cavern lay six male bodies, some still propped against the supports. The bodies were the source of the awful odor. They wore the uniforms of Cretan sailors.

"Shut in here while alive."

"Good riddance to them all!" Nereida spat at the sarcophagus. I tried to control my anger at this affront to my brother.

"At least the sailors got what they deserved," Cheon muttered. "They lied, and in turn were betrayed."

"What do you mean, 'they lied?'"

Tingas, who had been at the Athenian games, proceeded to tell me what had actually befallen Androgeos there. His tale was very much at odds with the one brought back by the sailors, the one that Ariadne had conveyed. According to Tingas, the night before the contests Androgeos invited his athletic rivals to a banquet at which he fed them a poison that weakened them enough to guarantee him victory the next day. Winning the laurels by this method was part of his attempt to overthrow Aegeus, which also included bribing port officials. One of those must have reported the plan to Aegeus. After the king was apprised, he, in Tingas's phrase, "cut off the Cretan snake's head before its body could exert its strength." The deed was done on the playing field, so it would be seen by many people, a smiting of Androgeos with the discus. Once Androgeos was dead, Aegeus ordered the Cretan sailors to take up their leader's body and with it return to Knossos.

In the tomb, whilst my comrades tapped at the walls and floor, seeking a route out, I pondered the implications of Tingas's version of Androgeos's death. On the Cretan sailors' way home, they must have concocted the tale that Ariadne later told to me, of our-brother-the-assassinated-hero, in the belief that if the sailors accurately recounted what had happened to Andro, Minos would kill them for not having prevented his son's death.

But why, then, did those sailors lay dead in this tomb? The only logical explanation was that Minos, realizing that the tale they told him was a lie, had them walled up here so that they could never change their story—and then he promoted as true the lie they had concocted, to manipulate the people of Crete into a frenzy for taking revenge on Athens for the death of their Cretan prince.

Once again I was forced to raise my estimate of the human capacity for deviousness. Angry, I bashed my horns against the nearest solid object, the sarcophagus, which broke its seal and jarred open its slate stone cover. The acrid chalk scent of limestone assaulted my nostrils, making me cough. Inside the coffin, the body's flesh had turned to dust and the bones were already disintegrating. Androgeos's royal burial garments had dissolved, except for a breastplate and some other metal objects. Picking up the skull, I dusted it off and sat down to contemplate the empty sockets.

"Alas, poor yokel! I never really knew him, Nereida, though he bore me on his back a thousand times."

"Don't be maudlin, Asterion. It's not becoming. Anyway, none of us ever gets to completely know another human being. How could we, when we're hardly able to know ourselves?" She reached into the sarcophagus, slipped a gleaming obsidian ring off a finger bone, dusted away the limestone, tried the ring on and admired it. She then passed it to Tingas and patted me on the withers as if sympathizing with my disconsolate surprise at the sailors' lie. "Let's scram, Asterion, before the lime rots us." Feeling somewhat the fool, I replaced Androgeos's skull at the top of his skeleton, closed the sarcophagus and exited the tomb.

The second of three corridor branches brought us to another dead end, one that yielded no hollow sound in the adjacent walls. Returning to the main trunk, we explored the last branch. Our supply of candles was near exhaustion and so were we, having spent two days in the tunnel without food, water, or sleep. Entry proved relatively easy: a door to be grasped and shoved aside into a niche of the structure that held the portal. That, combined with everything else I knew, made it a certainty that this was the final resting place of Queen Pasiphaë, high priestess of Crete.

"Mother, I salute you at last!"

There was no obvious trap at the door. I took that as evidence of haste on the part of the constructors and decorators. Of the nine panels that chronicled her life, the last was also empty—more evidence of haste. Knowing that the labyrinth above had been shuttered soon after her burial, I guessed that as a result of that premature closing, the priestesses who would otherwise have installed some sort of trap for the unwary and unworthy had been unable to complete that task. The lack of traps here and at Andro's tomb argued powerfully that Minos's soldiers had never penetrated this lower labyrinth.

This dark chamber wherein my mother's grave was laid was quite posh. Motifs from her life were arrayed on nine panels circling a hemispherical space, each separated from the next by carved support beams that ran up the walls and met at the center top. Here was Pasiphaë's descent from Helios, here her apprenticeship as priestess, her worship of the old Goddess and employment of the sacred snakes, her leadership of a procession for the funeral of Asterios, her betrothal to Minos. The panels pertaining to her children were the most densely detailed. I was not surprised that I had been omitted from the depictions of her offspring. Would I have figured on the blank ninth panel, or would that only have recorded her death?

At the center of the chamber stood the gisant, and below it, the coffin. Did that life-sized, recumbent figure of a woman atop Pasiphaë's coffin properly limn the features of my mother's face and figure? If so, it had been comely, with a certain long-leggedness to the torso that I had not inherited. She more resembled Phaedra than Ariadne and, for all of her alabaster iciness she was still sexy.

The stone gisant sported an emerald-green cloth robe and was bedecked by jewels on arms, hands, ankles, ears and forehead. Nearby to the coffin lay sealed chests of clothing, jewelry, rouges, polishes and oils. Nereïda and Xentha managed to open the chest of robes, plunge in their arms and come up with gowns whose luxuriousness made them gasp. Cheon and Tingas, with equal astonishment, sorted the jewelry cache. "Many, many fortunes," Cheon announced with reverence before he and Tingas, joined by Nereida and Xentha, cheerfully rooted about in the chests. Hunger and despair evaporated as they toyed with the jewelry and robes. Some treasures were native, others of exotic origin, gleaming with gemstones and filigreed metalwork. For a moment, these raiments transformed the Athenians into queens and kings, which they would never have become on the Peloponnese mainland. The remaining chests contained chalices, rhytons, amphorae, seals, statues, and amulets that had probably once been sequestered in the labyrinth and had been secreted here shortly before the priestesses were finally evicted from their temple.

Set into the walls were silver stanchions holding tarred sticks that would be lit to illuminate the vault during visitations. Cheon used a candle to set one tar torch ablaze. I shrank back, remembering how physician Enteros had scalded my leg. Emboldened by the brightness of the torch, Cheon, Tingas and Nereida closely examined the ceremonial gate that would have led outside. The portal was firmly shut; moreover, the light they shone through its chinks did not go far within. Rocks firmly blocked the exit.

Some day, stone by stone, patient diggers would remove those tons of impediments, enter, and try to decipher Queen Pasiphaë's life. And what would they find?

Shakespeare to the contrary notwithstanding, neither the good nor the evil that men (and women) do is interred with their bones. Our funereal dioramas are made to create legends, not to reflect the reality of a dead person's life. From the contents and décor of Pasiphae's tomb later generations would be led to infer a calm and logical procession through life of a queen of good breeding and high fashion sense, a woman whose existence centered on children, husband, worship of the Goddess, and on being properly decked out for all occasions. In the stylized renderings future generations would discover no hint of the passions that had truly ruled my mother's existence in the Middle

Realm. Where was the representation of her fierce love for the old, hairy-visaged Goddess of No Name, a love so strong that it had earned her punishment by Zeus and Poseidon? Where was the depiction of her humiliating but liberating voyage to Circe to obtain magic through which to chasten her errant husband? Where the montage of her Poseidon-inspired lust for the white bull, her insistence on giving birth to me, and her consequent holy death?

My musings were disturbed by the vulpine Xentha, shouting at Murex,

"What's wrong with wearing this necklace?"

"Suppose it was *your* mother's tomb," Murex said slowly, her beautiful face set hard. "You wouldn't want anyone stealing *your* mother's jewels."

"My mother has none. Maybe I'll take this home for her. And that, too," Xentha insisted, filching a second necklace from the cache and lifting it over her head.

"We're never going home!" Murex shouted.

"More reason to take what we want," Nereida chimed in.

"We're all going to die," Murex observed, and then collapsed tearfully on the edge of an unopened chest. "Do you think the gods cannot see our sacrilege?"

"There are no gods," Nereida said curtly. "There's only Asterion."

"I'm not a god, Nereida." Indeed, I had never felt less god-like than at the foot of my mother's sepulcher.

"You got a problem with us fondling her jewelry?"

"No. If playing with Pasiphaë's trinkets amuses you—go for it."

When we quit Pasiphaë's tomb to return to the upper labyrinth, Murex wore no jewels, but Xentha was heavy with bling and Nereida sported a necklace whose blue stones matched the hue of her eyes. Cheon carried the tar-torch and led the line, while Tingas, now wearing Androgeos's ring, brought up the rear.

Lost in bereaved thought about my mother, I hardly noticed as the footing became muddy; I merely marched in the midst of my companions, content to let others determine my path.

Then, in the deepest part of the cross-stream, they were suddenly on me! On top of me! Pushing me beneath the waters! Shoving the glaring hot torch at my disbelieving eyes! Stabbing at me with metallic blades! Why? Why? My death would be of no use to them! Fear collapsed inward, a weight on my heart. Gasping upward, I managed a mouthful of air but lost my footing and again submerged. Strength ebbed. Life narrowed. Water coursed through the labyrinth of my innards, water rose toward my ultimate hidden chamber, water blocked all exits, water quelled my storms and tried to make me into itself.

A watery death for a creature of Poseidon?

I broke the surface to call for help against my tormentors: "Water, close my wounds! Water, douse the torch! Water, upend my attackers!"

Roar, roar, and roar again! I shook the feeble humans from my hide, pierced them with horns more lethal than the daggers they stole from my brother's coffin. The earth moved beneath us. Waves of a different kind roiled the water, rattled the tunnel sides and ceiling, causing pieces to fall, making the mud treacherous.

"Let it come, let it come now, my father; I don't care if I die, but make them die with me!"

Stab. Thrust. Butt. Fling. Crush. Stomp. And above all: Roar.

The fighting stopped. The waves quieted. The tremors subsided. I clambered to a spot where the water was low enough to enable me to rest my hindquarters without submerging my torso. Breath heaved in and out of me, a world each time. Nereida was breathing, too, and shielding with her body a single lit candle. Murex leaned against the side of the cavern, her mouth agape but still breathing. Dead Cheon clutched the extinguished torch in one hand, a glinting blade in the other as his body floated on the turgid black waters toward the gate of the palace cistern. Dead Xentha's ankle was the only part of her extruding above water; her upper body was weighted to the muddy bottom by the queenly jewels she had stolen. Mortally wounded Tingas clutched at his gored abdomen. As blood seeped through his fingers, he looked questioningly at Murex; her perfection did not prevent his demise.

Later there would be time to deal with the mess. Later. I gathered Nereida and Murex and pushed them back toward the upper labyrinth. I yearned for higher and drier tunnels, familiar surroundings. Had the two women survivors taken active part in the attack, or had they merely been observers? Grateful for their companionship, I decided it no longer mattered.

The bedraggled Murex halted before the side corridor that led to the Childrens' Garden Cavern. "I want to have another look here."

"Some other time," I pleaded, but she shook her head, her tight curls flinging droplets of dark water to emphasize her resolve.

"More candles," Murex next demanded. Nereida yielded them after I nodded assent. What mattered a few candles now? Murex enfolded them in her mud-spattered tunic. The stream had wetted the cloth to her, rendering her body more curvaceous and appealing than ever. I looked forward to embracing her later, to find release from the day's carnage.

"Wait here," she instructed, and before we could react she trotted up the side corridor of hard-packed gravel and stood beneath the entrance portal to the catafalques and the pithoi filled with amber honey. The mechanism opened at the touch of her weight and she lifted herself up and inside. Immediately, the door shut below her.

"She forgot to set the stone counterweight," I blurted out and raced for the entrance, Nereida close behind me.

I stepped heavily on the place that would activate the entry device, but it did not move. Murex had not forgotten to set the counterweight. Rather, from the inside she had deliberately wedged the entrance shut, precluding us from rescuing her.

"What are you doing?" I shouted through the closed portal.

"Going. Home."

"You deceive yourself if you imagine that in there you will die gracefully, your body slowly weakening in the soft gleam of

86

hoarded candles until you pass out of life as gently as a child giving herself up to an afternoon nap. There will be terrible pain, awful despair. You will live only to spill bitterness over your remaining memories before death pinches out the candles. Come out! Stay with us!"

Again there was no answer.

"Watch. Out. For. Rats," Nereida warned.

Murex did not respond to that, either. Nereida and I waited awhile to see if she would change her mind, but when we reached the last of our candles and she still remained silent, we left Murex to her lingering suicide.

There ensued for Nereida and me an elegiac time. Her eyes gleamed with triumph at having accomplished what I had once laughed at her for suggesting: she had helped me with the others and I had not killed her. Oikolos had been a better sexual partner, and Murex more desirable, but Nereida proved to be the most adept at reacting to her surroundings, and she became mistress of the labyrinth.

When we could bear it we made excursions to the lower tunnels. We couldn't get at Murex, and Cheon's body had floated downstream to lodge against the gate of the cistern. No Meat there. We brought back the undecomposed flesh of Xentha and Tingas for storage, and tried to eat of it sparingly. In the lower tunnel complex, we discovered routes to other tombs and caches, but did not explore them, as these were even less likely to yield an exit. Nereida appropriated several of Pasiphaë's gowns and pieces of jewelry, claiming that I became more sexually adventurous when she wore my mother's garments.

With our new understanding of the maze as mortuary, we were able to identify various chambers and equipment in the upper labyrinth. Here was the Drying Room, where gutted bodies were drained and dusted with a preservative powder. The Canopicary contained odd-shaped ollas designed to hold internal organs while the priestesses examined them for predictive possibilities. The Mummifactorum had cloth fragments strewn about, and a profuse supply of amulets for insertion in the folds of the cloths to be wrapped around a dead person.

At mid-day, from the Navel we watched the transit of the sun. We exercised and ran about in the Vaulted Arena. We passed a night in the Onion, another hard by the Lionhead Fountain, a third shivering in the Cruelest Chamber. In Poseidon's Cone she listened respectfully to the sound of the earth, but did not hear the god's voice as I did, though she was polite enough not to comment. Of all the rooms, I kept Nereida only from the Cone Descendent, though I entered there frequently to check for signs from Ariadne. Occasional bits of food and flowers had been dropped to the floor, but no message announced an imminent visit. That was fine with me.

The ribs we licked became too frequently chewed, the cracked thigh bones, empty of marrow. We roamed from chamber to chamber, seeking relief from the heat, finally settling near the Lionhead Fountain, with its lightly bubbling waters. Lethargy sat on our shoulders.

"Just when I've come to know what I want out of life," Nereida said, "all possibilities will be taken from me. Better that I had never been born."

"If you died at birth, or never lived, you would never have known anything about the world. No sensations, no feelings, no memories."

"Which of my sensations should I cherish, Asterion? Betrayal by my king? Anguish at watching my friends die? Happiness at overcoming nausea to eat their flesh? Triumph at remaining alive a few weeks longer than the others? No, Asterion, I'm glad to be going, for my suffering will soon end. Yours, however, will only worsen. Those whom you have killed already dance in the shadows of your eyes."

"I eat because hunger drives me."

"Your will to go on living despite the emotional cost is your glory and your burden. Poor Asterion. Do you know that I have tried to love you?"

"I accept what you say, though I don't know what love is—one of my many failures of understanding, I'm sure."

"Love is an expression of willingness to belong to another."

"Like a slave or a captive?"

"No, Asterion. Like being proud and humble at feeling so deeply. I have tried to love you, not because you are worthy of love, but because I am."

"That I don't understand either."

"To be human is to have the opportunity to experience love, to really love someone, before one dies. It's the ultimate in emotions. How I envy Xentha and Cheon, who loved one another so completely and died together."

I shook my head and horns, unable to confirm, deny, or even comment meaningfully on her contentions.

"Time for sex," Nereida insisted, and without waiting for my assent threw herself at me and caressed me in ways that she knew aroused me. Slow-paced at first, our copulation became intense. She gripped me with a fierce power and I was glad not to resist. I thrust for all the beautiful young men and women, for the ethereal Iola, the spunky Oikolos, Murex behind her wall, Xentha and her valiant Cheon, Tingas the eternal follower, Ptach the overly inquisitive, for them and for the others whose names I never learned, those who, indeed, as she had accused, danced now only in the shadows of my eyes; I thrust to make Nereida feel beyond feeling; I thrust out of pity at my loveless state.

At last she reached an explosive, long-anticipated but still overwhelming climax that brought tears to her eyes and her whisper to my ear: "Now, Asterion! Do it now!"

Seven

I destroy, therefore I am?

Perhaps. But if so, I wasn't terribly good at my job, nor had I made a reality that was congruent enough with my fantasies.

Would I have had a better time, prior to killing my victims, if I'd first forced them to act as I instructed them? Certainly! So, as I awaited the next set of sacrifices, and based on my determination to fashion more satisfying sexual and murderous experiences, I concocted new dramas for them that featured slow torture and pyramiding horror. My ruminations on these future playlets were interrupted by odd sensations: of peering out from a farmer's hearth at twilight, of standing on the deck of a fishing vessel and rolling with the steep waves of a summer storm, of my loins seeping with vaginal flow: remembrances of someone else's times past. I was vast; I contained multitudes—or at least, multiple images of yesteryears. And this, five thousand years before Virtual Reality headsets.

But the darkness was getting to me. Its shadows matched those in my mind. To escape both I visited the Navel when the sun was directly above, and found a bonus, for in the thin soil of the canyon floor some shoots were growing, pale onions, sweet grass, carrots, crocuses. I plucked up a carrot, nibbled at it, and amazed my mouth. The nice little crunch of stalk, its sweet juices more vitalizing than water! Alas, there were not enough of these mini-veggies to dissuade me from continuing to imagine my next Meat-based repast.

Vulture feathers had also drifted to this garden, from aeries way up on the canyon; I stuck several feathers in my matted mane. Later, with this plumage still in place, I traipsed through the Mirrorgate into the lower labyrinth, seeking other adornment. Long before I reached the underground stream that fed the palace, the smell of Cheon's decaying corpse wafted to me. As I moved closer to the nexus I heard sounds: the clank of metal against metal, the slosh of objects through water, the dull thud of an implement striking flesh. Candles aloft, I slogged through the low-lying stream, and recognized ahead a familiar shape.

"Is that you, Daedalus?"

"Yes, Asterion. And we must speak low."

Daedalus sat inside the cistern grate, on a rope-and-basket sling similar to the one that now and then lowered Ariadne into the labyrinth, and lit by a candelabrum perched above him in the grating. He was attempting to cut into small pieces the remains of Cheon's bloated, half-hacked body, which the current had wedged against the grate. The decaying corpse had been polluting the palace's water supply, and Daedalus was trying to make smaller pieces to be lifted up and out for disposal.

"Help me in this task, Asterion," Daedalus said, and held out to me a sharp blade. I grasped a handle. We worked at the corpse, he on his side of the impenetrable grate and I on mine.

"Two captives, sawing and hacking."

"You a captive, Daedalus? Since when?"

"It began after Cyclade's death."

"I hadn't known that your wife was that gravely ill. I'm sorry."

"My workshop had always been in the palace, and shortly after Cyclade's death Icarus and I were invited to reside in the palace—I yielded to the argument that the boy wouldn't be quite as lonely or miss his mother so much if he and Phaedra could spend more time together. A week after I moved in, Enteros suggested that I send an assistant to the port to buy silver rather than make the journey myself—another good idea, one that saved me time. A few days on, when I set out to stroll in the outer gardens, the eunuchs informed me that henceforth I must confine my walks to the interior."

"Minos twisted your better instincts. Why am I not surprised? Do you and Ariadne share a room?"

"We do not, and don't fixate on that, Asterion. You and I have other business together—isn't that why you left this rotting message? I once sent a signal in a similar way, although I was not aware that I was signaling."

"The nephew that you killed on the mainland?"

"My rival, maker of toys far more lifelike than mine—too clever by half, that young man." Daedalus was grim-lipped at the memory.

Cheon's body was all in pieces, now, and easily pushed through the grate to Daedalus's side. Soon the artificer would have to tug the rope, or those above would suspect an attempt at escape and come down to investigate.

"Daedalus," I importuned him, "send me seeds. Rooting vegetables. Anything that will grow with a minimum of light."

"And you, Asterion, give me those feathers in your mane. And gather others and send them to me during Ariadne's visits."

"Her visits are more rare than the plumes. Are you two planning an escape?"

"I will go in the only direction possible from this island, Asterion: through the sky. But not Ariadne. Her destiny is here, as is yours."

By the time that a new group of fourteen virgins arrived in my labyrinth, I was so frantic with hunger that I dispatched the first few of them too quickly. Recovering my aplomb, I was able to ravish several of the females, and I avoided another of my first-batch mistakes by not becoming too emotionally involved with the remaining captives. I could not, because my main objective was to make my Meat last. Perhaps my failure to get involved was the basis of my sense that this second set of fourteen were not as joyous as the first set had been. They seldom laughed. I missed Nereida, and it was little consolation that she was within me.

When this B-team was all gone, hunger returned, and it seemed to do so more rapidly than it had after the first batch. I subsisted on water, and waited. And waited, and waited, a-throb with hunger, suspended between life and death, shaken by violent dreams.

Looking past the frightening aspects of those dreams, I found them to be instructive. They showed me a way of killing quickly so as to not spoil my main sources of nutrition, the muscles of the torso, thighs, and upper arms. The technique involved stomping the human head. When the third set of victims arrived, I practiced on them, and found head-stomping to be very methodical and efficient—except that I had to do it so quickly that I eliminated the possibilities of sexual satisfaction. Not liking that trade-off very much, I decided in the future to give up some efficiency for the sake of pleasure.

The weather turned colder. Hotter. Wetter. Drier. I came to know the labyrinth so well that I hardly needed my eyes to navigate it. The maze was a part of me, my external entrails. As I counted the days until the next batch of sacrifices should arrive—I figured that they were coming in tune with the spring and fall solstices—I hunkered down in the Cone of the Disappearing Ceiling, the Funnel Ascendant.

Some days later—truthfully, I had lost track of time—I became aware of the noise and aroma of the descending rope and basket. The candles illumined a woman whose beauty had burnished in the past year.

"You look ravishing, Ariadne. New jewelry of exotic origin?"

"You are correct, Asterion."

"It becomes you. And I see that a more commodious conveyance has been arranged for you by your lover."

"The basket is easier to sit in. Actually, Asterion, my affair with Daedalus began out of my gratitude for him helping me visit you."

"Is that so?"

"It is."

She strode about the circular chamber in a sensuous,

self-assured manner, hips undulating, breasts fluttering at each step. Her bell skirt was interwoven with strands of gold that gleamed in the candles' glow. Her black and silver facial accents were bolder than ever. Murex would have lost the contest to this princess!

"There was no point in saving myself for a handsome prince from abroad. Anyway, there are none whose power even faintly approaches that of Minos, and he would never agree to an alliance for me with a man far beneath my station."

"Your sisters married minor gods."

"It's a choice. But really, Asterion, could you see me cooped up in a dusty old temple with nobody for company but hags and eunuchs?"

"No. Your carnality is quite pronounced."

"Do you have sex with all the females before you kill them?"

I bowed. "Is that why you asked me to kill them all quickly? To prevent me from having sex with them?"

"They must die so that something new may be born. With each death you grow stronger, Asterion. You don't realize your power: you are the center of the Minoan Empire."

"Do you glory in that empire, Ariadne? The servants, the pomp, the luxuries, the sense of awe that you command?"

"I hate it."

My laughter rang off the conical walls and caused Ariadne's cheeks to flush. She raised her hand as if to attack me.

"Go ahead. Then I'll have to grab you to defend myself, and who knows what would happen next?"

She lowered her hand. "For now I accept Minos's gifts and the comfort they provide, Asterion, but I yearn to avenge my mother, my brother, and all those innocents whom my father has sent to their deaths. I long for the day when you, Asterion, call upon Poseidon to bring down the kingdom of Minos—when ships sink, mountains erupt, and the earth opens up and swallows the tyrant! On that day, Asterion my brother, you and I will be free."

"Faugh! We'll be buried beneath the rubble along with

everyone else. And what makes you think that I can entreat Poseidon to bring down Minos and his empire? I do not presume that the god would ever do my bidding."

"I repeat: You do not know your own strength."

"I kill when hunger overtakes me and I cannot staunch the urge to stay alive."

Anxious ripples came from the dangling rope: Daedalus must have sensed danger approaching.

"I kiss your hand," Ariadne said, and gave a soft embrace of her dark-lined lips. I planted a like kiss on her palm, my lips now far larger than her entire hand.

"Oh, I almost forgot," she said as she climbed into the rope and basket and started aloft. From it she tossed me a small, metallic device. "Daedalus sent this for you. He hasn't harvested any seeds yet, but said you'd know what to do with this."

The device was a pair of bronzed gimbals, two rings pivoted on axes at right angles to one another; the smaller one swinging freely inside the larger. I remembered the feathers for Daedalus, and tossed them into the rapidly receding basket. Ariadne's bell skirt vanished upward into the darkness.

After the last pheromes of her scent dispersed, I began to twirl the undulating gimbals. A sudden frisson swept up my backbone and tickled my brain: the gimbals were Daedalus and I, each suspended in a prison, free only to move within it. The gift held my eyes. At that moment, I knew, Daedalus was directly above, working the lift machinery that he had created, sweating with exertion as it raised Ariadne from her sojourn in the depths, up and through the hole in the floor of her bedchamber ...

Ariadne steps lightly from the basket onto solid tile, gives me a quick embrace and brushes my cheek with her painted lips, then hurries me from her chamber. I limp through the dim corridors toward my own quarters, appearing as though nothing has happened and nothing will ever happen. Ariadne does not love me, I know, but I am content to be the current focus of the yearning gleam that never leaves her eyes, a gleam that—shades of Pasiphaë!—promises unrelenting wildness. Asterion would be better suited to such lascivious rutting as Ariadne imagines, a lust for abandon itself, for oblivion.

Icarus, my golden boy, at play with mock sword and shield! Handsome where I am ugly, athletic and supple where I am only strong—the ultimate mystery of a man's life lies not in his vocation or his gods or his choice of spouse, but in the maturing of his child. I am not as able to bend my flesh and blood child as I am the materials in my workshop. There, wood on the lathe is my bone, liquid metal in the forge my blood, twisted rope my sinew, pottery and glass my congealed breath.

Asterion is the unseen terror of the empire, but I, Daedalus, I am its secret engine, creator of cages within cages.

The poor Minotaur thinks that Minos has kept him from returning to his youthful placid cud-chewing. How misguided. Asterion has yet to admit that he is fulfilling the destiny to which his shape and substance condemned him at his birth. He is as dependent on Minos for his continued existence, as Minos is on the Minotaur to frighten and sustain his empire.

The chain linking Minos to Minotaur is unbreakable and eternal.

The two stare at one another across the chasm at the nether edge of the Middle Realm, across an abyss of bile, a gorge rimmed with calcified tears and shadows of stunted trees and monstrous jagged seashells. This is where the infant Zeus was spirited when Cronos sought to destroy him. Minos is resplendent in purple, his beard flecked with white, his voice plaintive:

"Great Zeus, I have compelled obeisance from every land of the Cycladean archipelago and the Peloponnese mainland. At Crete every vessel disgorges the fruits of the earth and of the seas and of the labors of man. But I shall not rest until the peace of Zeus is absolute.

"The Minotaur was a brilliant stroke, Great Zeus, the finest example of Thy grand command of human affairs. Although at first I resented the creature, I have, as instructed, turned him to advantage. But he can and will do more to complete the sacred task

entrusted to me, the final banishment from the Middle Realm of the
Goddess of No Name.

"Never again, Great Zeus, the unthinking worship of the change of the seasons! Never again, the presumptuous tyranny of priestesses! Never again, women's power to enslave us! Men will rule! All hail Zeus, Poseidon, and Hades!"

I roar, a roar that echoes from stalactite to stalagmite, up, down, around, and back again among the vast, shadowed caverns, a roar that sets a-tremble the limestone projections, that knocks fragile spires into piles of stones. Boulders strike at me, beat me down, threaten to bury me. Have I become lord of the labyrinth only to smother beneath a pile of stones in Zeus's Nursery? At least Minos will die with me! Oh, the apt symmetry of simultaneous perishing! A rock smashes at my head. Lightning obscures my vision.

The trembling of the earth has stopped. Shaking off the stones and the many blows I have sustained, I make my way among the subterranean caverns toward a light beckoning from beyond. I hear only the soughing of the winds in these depths, and the murmuring of the stream. With difficulty I clamber toward a shaft of light. Can freedom be so near? After all that has happened, can release be so simple? With a few dozen strides I attain the edge of the cavern and push aside a last few rocks between me and the outside. As I shove these, a flash of light winks at me. The sun. The sun.

What a graceless body I now have: creaky, adipose, tongue-tied. Emerging from the cavern, I am met by eunuchs from the palace, who are overjoyed to see me and who seem to expect solemn silence from me in the wake of my visit to Zeus's Nursery. They assist me into a sedan chair. I am borne away. Along the roads, shepherds and farmers bow low. Food is passed to me. I eat it without savor. I run my hands—gloriously uncloven!—over the wood of the sedan chair. I lean out to inhale the flowers, but they have no perfume. As we enter the palace, beauteous maidens and comely men are everywhere; I recognize their beauty but feel no urge to possess them sexually. Even Ariadne, who prostrates herself at my feet and embraces my legs in tearful welcome, does not arouse me. I stroke her hair.

Evening draws nigh. I am ushered into a cushioned chamber with a soft bed, and left alone. Guards stand just outside—to keep intruders out or to keep me in? I try to give this body up to sleep, but a knot in my shoulder is a plot a-hatching, a lower back pain is a revolt brewing, a sour breath is the emanation from secret priestesses lighting candles and fondling snakes. All traitors must be watched, all watchers spied upon, all spies hunted down so that they will not reveal their secrets.

After dawn finally breaks, I wander the corridors and rooms of the palace. At every step I take, courtiers and visitors bow before me, flatter me, and present me with gifts. Yet I know that any of them, given the opportunity, will take my life. Emblems of labyrinth and Minotaur are everywhere, some sketchy, like the glyphs on the coins, others more detailed. There are no likenesses of King Minos, only of the heads of bulls.

Daedalus is at his forge. "Welcome, my king! I am proud that you have chosen to visit the smithy and carpentry shop so early in the day. A thousand times welcome! My newest project, sire—let me pull it from the forge. There! A mirror, your highness, but no ordinary one, for it shows not only the likeness of the face but also of the rear of the head—what is behind you as well as what is in front."

Refusing to glance in it, I hurry from the artificer's lair, only to encounter in the halls another shock: Phaedra. The fair-haired, cherubic waif has become a gangling, prepubescent girl, her cheeks still flushed with excitement, her hair not a whit less golden, but her future womanhood already palpable. Why do the years go so quickly?

Nobles and courtiers gather around the throne. One dances, another sings, a third plays lyres and flutes, a fourth mimes a mock Minotaur frightening sacrifices.

I determine to walk in the palace's gardens, and stroll outside. Of all things in the Middle Realm, the Minotaur has yearned most for this simple pleasure.

It is joyless. I see the flowers but cannot smell them, and the pain in my back counters my urge to bend and touch them.

It is unnecessary for me to move much or to speak, since the daily business of the palace goes on regardless of what I do or do not do.

The eunuchs guard what must be guarded, the clerks catalogue the commerce, the cooks prepare meals, and the cleaners whisk and tidy the chambers. When there are decisions I must make, I make them in silence. I reject with a gesture a supplicant request from a visiting minor Egyptian pharaoh; on the spot, he doubles the amount that Egypt is willing to pay. Dismissed! When an underling dares ask a question or seek direction, I scowl as though the answer should be obvious. Dismissed! A drawn plan of an ancillary palace is shown; I open my arms to convey that its dimensions must be enlarged. Dismissed! A fine cow from the palace herd is displayed, as though to be killed for Meat; I pardon her and send her back to the pasture. Against my steward's recommendation I order wine distributed to the farmers. Power is choosing what may flourish and what will be allowed to decay. If I create a city here, then over there one shall fall into desuetude. If I allow certain subjects to live freely, then others will have to be enslaved.

That is why the supplicant nations give me a few of their youth—in the hope that my power will then leave the rest of their young people unharmed. Terror is surprisingly easy to administer. Terror allows me to frighten people into submission without any need to offer them any positive promises.

Into my reception chamber come a set of potential sacrifices, newly arrived from the wharf, fourteen fine-looking youths and maidens in shackles, a mixed batch, not from Athens this time but from the islands that lie between Crete and the Mycenaean mainland, from the Phoenician cities of Sidon and Tyre, from the Lydian coast, and from Cyrenaica in the desert. Their variety will provide a bit of stimulation for my Minotaur, and their presence in the rotation will mean we need to demand less frequent tribute from Athens, which will make it harder for Aegeus to incite his people to revolt against me.

Seated once more in a sedan chair, I lead a grand progression of the captives toward the exterior of the labyrinth. An enormous crowd of citizens and nobles follows me. The anemones are in flower, their ornate tendrils threading the air like kite strings. We approach the labyrinth.

Dozens of eunuchs with double-axes station themselves just outside the maze, ready to slash at anything that emerges, whilst others pry open the entrance and expose the translucent corridor. I half expect the Minotaur to emerge and attack me, but there is no movement from within. What fearful noises come from the captives as they are thrust through the entrance and the great door is quickly closed behind them! Their fright is such that they cannot prevent awful sounds from escaping their lips. The crowd of watchers outside the labyrinth does not disperse but remains at the translucent wall, waiting to see the Minotaur dispatch the sacrifices.

There! She went through the sixth door on the left—that will take her into the Onion. I'll get to that chamber first! Ah, the scent of quarry! Ah, the blood hunger! I am the lord of the labyrinth! The Minoan Empire depends on me!

Eight

My fellow dwellers in the House of Hades, it will not, I trust, diminish the suspense of my tale to inform you that my next years in the labyrinth were filled with a cornucopia of sacrificial victims, boatloads from wherever the Cycladean Seas—excuse me, the Minoan Seas!—lapped ashore.

I became an expert in producing death: a practiced and inexorable assassin; an anatomist able to empty prime arteries with a flick of a horn or a snap of a jaw; and a facilitator hastening the sacrifices' spirits into Netherworld while making their bodies part of mine. Their presence within me was so palpable that I knew which one had lodged in my pancreas, which in my third stomach, and which in my cloven right hoof. To avoid being overwhelmed by my victims' memories, after a while I ceased eating their brains. I preferred my own memories, so that during the endless days between the arrivals of new victims I could relive past gories.

One impression was shared by many of the sacrifices: the profoundly corrupting influence of Minos's blood tax on the peoples of the Minoan Sea. Where once upon a time adolescents had admired their ripening bodies in mirrors and through the appraising glances of the opposite sex, now those maturing children and their parents were all too aware that ineluctable blossoming would bring the most beauteous of adolescents to the attention of those gathering the sacrifices. Nobody wanted to win this version of *Athenian Idol*. Parents disfigured their progeny, exiled their sons and daughters to foreign lands, and bribed officials to pass by their houses. "Mirror, mirror on the wall, who's the fairest of them all? I hope it ain't me!" To avoid being in the Final Fourteen, children touted to the collectors their schoolmates' handsomeness and winsome behavior.

An indiscriminate labrys, the blood tax sundered relationships, stole wealth, and compelled criminality. Deliberately foul and coercive behavior oozed into every nook and cranny of the Minoan Empire. Each island, each colony, each village became a nest of espionage, betrayal, and extortion. Local authorities often chose more than fourteen victims so as to extract money from parents for de-listing this one or that one, even to goading the parents to have their children enslaved, arguing to them that a life of misery was better for their children than being killed by the monster, even if such a death was pre-certified as holy.

Deviance was continually being defined downward. By a half-decade into Minos's rule, bribery, lying, informing, and bullying were no longer practiced only by the nobility—the middleclass were all-in, as were the poor. Neighbor betrayed neighbor not for a small fortune but for a basket of eggs; everyone lied so reflexively that no one any longer knew what truth was, and ordinary people began to value only what had been obtained by deceit (an action heretofore only the province of rulers). Artistry ceased, lest it call attention to its creators as gifted. Commerce languished. The only cooperation was among thieves. Relations between men and women were shorn of tenderness; all that remained were trades.

As the arrival of my food supply became more reliable and the intervals between sets of sacrifices more predictable, I altered my treatment of the captives. When a new group first appeared, to blunt my hunger and to establish the right tone I quickly killed a few, deliberately in front of the other captives. While the remainder were stupefied, I organized them in such a way as to assure that as many as possible stayed alive for as long as possible.

To prevent their ganging up on me, I allowed the captives to explore and exploit the various tombs reachable through the lower labyrinth—there were more than I'd previously discovered—and to retrieve costumes, trinkets, devices and hidden caches of olive oil and honey that could assist us in sexual experimentation.

We were a sexual court that meted out rewards and punishments, a temple that fostered shameful private practices, a brilliantly innovative brothel, a counting house with live coin, a farm on which forbidden liaisons were encouraged, an army barracks in which obedience was an art form. My captives' suppleness, strength, and imagination came to the fore, and as a group we surpassed ourselves in switching partners until we became one gigantic, interconnected, self-stimulating organism, continually engaged in the sublime task of fulfilling what the Archangel Freud would identify as our polymorphous propensities.

Having world enough and time, in addition to sexual experimentation we tried various forms of governance. Kingship proved the easiest to arrange, since I was so clearly in charge and the captives were already trained in submission; but once in a while I would suspend my regal rights and give in to the group's urges for everyone to be equal, or some other anti-hierarchical nonsense. Yes, nonsense! My fellow shades, you know and I know that all men and women are created unequal. We are unequal in appearance, talent, strength, intelligence, capacity for management, endurance, resilience, whatever. Therefore, any attempts at giving to each person an equal say in their governance is inherently doomed to failure. The only truth of universal inequality is this maxim: From each, despite their needs, to each, according to their abilities.

How did Karl Marx get that so backwards?

The captives, given the option of existing in mixed company or in all-male and all-female clusters, did the latter. I stayed mostly with the men, since the women chattered so endlessly. We males always wondered: Were the gals talking about our shortcomings? Of how to make us do their bidding? We guys were upset at hearing the murmurs of the distaff crew, and we were bothered even more by their occasional, deafening silences.

What were the gals up to? Was it female-on-female sex, as per-fected on the nearby Isle of Lesbos? Did women know better how to excite one another than we men knew how to arouse them? We couldn't be certain, because when they emerged from their private sessions, they just glanced knowingly at each other.

The all-male groups also surprised me. I fancied that such gangs would feature fewer instances of homoerotic behavior than the females; in matters sexual I greatly favored female part-ners and assumed that the other guys did, too. When because of the need to be reciprocally polite I occasionally found it nec-essary to have sex with a male, I did so reluctantly, and when required to be the haven for a rambunctious penis, closed my eyes and thought of empire.

More disturbing was the tendency among males to isolate our group in a large room, there to light a fire and stomp around it while beating out a rhythm on the bottoms of ollas, and after-wards to tearfully admit to one another how deeply we missed our fathers and brothers. Not having known my true father and having had only fleeting contact with Androgeos, I remained silent when they attributed their inadequacies to bad familial role models. At times induced to join circular confessional con-fraternities, I drew the line at teaching my new brothers how to roar, telling them that articulate speech was one of the glories of being human.

"Don't be so smugly superior," a Lycian farmer spat at me during one feeling-drenched fireside encounter. "We all need friends to help us get by. Don't you?"

"Asterion doesn't have friends," another celebrant accused.

"You are all my friends."

"Quit hiding behind those horns, Asterion! If you have a single friend in this world, tell us who it is."

"Daedalus."

"He's not in the labyrinth. Name some other friends."

"Alright. There was Nereida, and to a lesser extent Oikolos, and—"

"Are all of your friends captive women? Don't you like men?

Don't you trust us? Don't you want to hear what we have to say? Or share our problems, our joys, our fears? Do you think we can't understand *your* problems?" This guy named Panthus, this Lycian farmer, kept at me: "You really don't want us to be your friends, because if we are your friends then you won't be able to bring yourself to eat us."

"That could be true, but since none of you are very much like me, you'll never know what it is to be me or to have my problems."

"Am I less unique than you?" Panthus pressed on. "I'm alive. I'm intelligent and sensitive and caring and sexy. And I'm shut up in the labyrinth and can't escape."

"There are many human beings, but there's only one Minotaur!"

Panthus leaned back in satisfaction. "An arrogant answer, Asterion, and one that could as well have come from Minos, whom you say that you hate. You demean us just as Minos does, by refusing to consider us as your equals. You both stink."

Panthus burned brightly, and like a flame attracted many to his heat. In him I saw my long-dead brother Androgeos and, although the sensation was not fully formed, I also saw in Panthus the spark of he who would come one day to slay me. Perhaps that was why I permitted Panthus to become the last of his group to survive. When we had shared the Meat of the penultimate victim, I thanked him for having taught me about life.

"Bah, Asterion," he said, "It's easy to skewer another's foibles. It's much harder to love them, faults and all, and without pity. I'm unable to do that. I adore the great mass of people but detest every single individual I've ever known. I cry but don't ache, regret but don't mourn. At least I do not yield to chaos."

"I agree with you on all of those things. Maybe you're just as much a potential mass killer as I am an actual one."

I think Panthus became my friend, but since I don't know much about having a friend or being one, I can't really say. Surely, friendship is not that oafish good fellowship of back-slapping and trading stories about female bitchiness and male bravado that came to the fore when we males sat around a fire. Is friendship the sharing of confidences? Doing small services for one another, a matter of reciprocity? Does friendship have to be put to a test before it becomes meaningful? Will a real friend let you to lie to yourself? Permit you to change? Insist on it? If to be in love is to be blind, to be a good friend surely requires wide-open eyes.

I killed Panthus and ate his brain and testicles, hoping to inculcate his intelligence and passion. For a while afterwards his mocking voice rang in my ears, tweaking me for arrogance. Panthus's impatience at the stupidity of the Middle Realm jostled in my brain alongside Nereida's fond view of her mother on the doorstep of a rude hut in twilight, and Cheon's ecstasy at his first horseback ride.

There were no victims left, and there had been none for far longer than I had become used to. My hunger returned so strongly that I could not even sit still. I paced from one room to another. The Onion, the Rogalhida, the Cruelest Chamber, Twin Ollas, Reciprocal Snakes, the Eighty-First, the Disappearing Ceiling, the Navel, the Lionhead Basin, the Corridor of Yes Maybe No, the Umbilical, Three Basins, and the Vaulted Arena, until I came to Poseidon's Cone, where, exhausted, I sat to rest.

Listening to the tide burbling below, to the other creaks and secret whispers of the earth, I tried to understand myself and my wretched existence by reference to what I had learned from my captives about the lives of my half-brothers, Poseidon's other "monstrous" offspring. Don't we all want to know more about our crazy relatives that we've never met? Why else, the 21st century zeal for genealogy? I had seven demigod half-brothers. Only three had aught to do with the sea. Triton, surpassingly ugly, rode through the waves on the backs of sea beasts. Also seagoing were Otus and Ephailtes, giants each taller than the largest human-made edifice; they could not be killed except by each other—which, of course, condemned them to eternal fratricidal combat.

Pegasus, that flying horse, was sired by Poseidon out of snake-tressed Medusa, she whose glance turned flesh to stone. It was beyond me what my true father could have seen in that death-dealing harridan. But knowing of Pegasus's godly DNA, I was dismayed at the profound docility of the flying horse—he was willing to allow Bellerophon to bridle and ride him while exacting nothing in return. And he was the only half-brother of mine who did not kill humans.

I regret to say that most of my half-brothers were incredibly stupid. Consider one-eyed Polyphemus: He ate a sextet of men at one sitting, but then became drunk, which allowed Odysseus, whom he had captured, to take the occasion to blind Polyphemus's remaining eye and escape. Later, blind Polyphemus crushed Acis, his rival for the nymph Galatea—as if that would make her love him instead!

Love: it's what undid nearly all of the demigods. Take Orion, the great hunter, also a half-brother of mine. In the Middle Realm an indiscriminate killer of fawns and gazelles, in romantic matters he was mostly a rapist until he fell for Eos, goddess of the dawn. Now there's a self-defeating passion! For Eos spent only a few brief moments with Orion each day before vanishing. Frustrated, Orion pursued the Pleiades sisters, which finally proved to be too much for Apollo, who wanted those maids for himself, and the new sun-god set a giant scorpion to pursue Orion toward the sea, and then tricked Artemis into shooting her arrows at both the hunter and the hunted, killing both Orion and Scorpio, turning them into neighboring constellations.

To shine forever in the night sky: Not a bad fate, all things considered.

Of the seven half-brothers I was most intrigued by Antaeus, the giant of the Libyan Desert, whose strength was absolute so long as he was in direct touch with the earth, which was of course the fiefdom of his mother, Gaea. Talk about clinging to Mom's apron strings! Still, I admired his tenacity, his capacity for regeneration, his ability to shift moods. A good candidate for enshrinement in the heavens, wouldn't you think? But his death was ignominious—held aloft by Heracles and crushed to death in a bear hug—and his posthumous fate was to be scattered about as dust.

And what was his sin? Existing.

As far as the gods are concerned, no matter what you do they'll condemn you for it. The gods have created so many categories of sins that it is almost impossible for the rest of us demigods and human beings not to transgress one or another, even when we're being very careful. Take sex, for example: under certain circumstances sex is a sin, yet not under others. Define your terms, you gods! But of course they won't. They deliberately leave 'em vague, so there'll be something to catch us for.

Here's a list of ten sins that I committed: Murder. Theft. Adultery. Covetousness. Lust. Pride. Refusal to worship the gods. Dishonoring my parents. Cannibalism. Torture. Guilty! Very, very guilty!

Now *you*, my fellow shades, have probably only committed one or two of those sins. So you're not so bad. But you're not so good as to have gotten yourselves sent to the Elysian Fields yet, are you? No, of course not. But take heart: Very few get there on the first go-around.

Why did the gods create human sin? Not simply because they could—no, no, their motivation was even more basic: the gods created sin because they envied human beings.

Envied for what? For being mortal, of course! Humans use an understanding of their eventual death as a basis for sensitivity, empathy, and love for fellow human beings, and to muster more resilience to adversity than the gods can ever summon. What is it that Christians admire about Jesus? Or Buddhists about the Buddha? Their godly parts? No! It is their all-too-human aspects. You don't see the Greek gods turning the other cheek as Jesus did, do you? Or meditating their way out of a jam, à la Buddha? Humans build ideas, institutions, and identities. The gods do not. Humans look after their partners, participate in families, rear their children, care for their aged—and they do it all out of love! The gods do not. The gods' deepest emotions are envy, lust, and the will to exercise power. To be human is to be *beyond* divine. The gods know that; it is why they continually punish humanity.

I roared the pain of being at least partly human at Poseidon, roared until there began a trembling in the earth and a protesting groan from the depths, as though Poseidon was being forced to lash out if only to quiet my voice.

After a while the tremors stopped; but the sequence of roar and rapid response proved to me the correctness of Ariadne's contention that I had the power to summon Poseidon's wrath. I did not use the power just then, confused as to whether doing so would avail me in the Netherworld to which I would have to descend, or whether it would countervail the onus of my having killed, one by one, so many youths that I'd already lost count. I was content to believe that at some future date I could summon a Poseidon-instigated upheaval and let it provide me with a fitting death, one that would command the respect of the gods and all their creatures. No one could ask for anything more.

Next day, calmer, while strolling near the Chamber of the Disappearing Ceiling I heard the familiar mechanical noise of the descending apparatus. And for the first time I did not await Ariadne with eagerness. Much as I loathed my isolation, there was a certain comfort in being answerable in it to no one, and especially not to a woman so powerfully able to affect me as Ariadne. Thus it was with a sense of relief that I recognized the person being lowered into my domain as Phaedra.

"Hi," Phaedra smiled, as though we'd last seen one another moments ago. "Brought you some stuff." From the folds of her jacket she pulled handfuls of sweetcakes and held them out to me. I quickly put them in my mouth, out of hunger but also from a wish to occupy my jaws so I would not have to speak. By her actions and demeanor she was a girl still, but her body had rounded and curved toward full womanhood, and she was desirable.

"Daedalus wants to know if you have any more feathers."

My mouth full of honey, I wondered momentarily if Phaedra had become a rival to Ariadne for the attentions of the old artificer, then concluded that her suitor would more likely be her age-mate, Icarus. Having anticipated this Daedalian request, I had cached the feathers in an olla and now fetched them for her. "Terrif!," she gushed as she transferred the feathers into the basket of the rope apparatus. "We've been collecting some, and making them temporarily into fans, so nobody'll know what they're for."

"Who is we?"

"Me and Icky."

"You two still best buds?"

Rather than retreating up the rope immediately, Phaedra sat for a while, unable to resist talking about her favorite subject. Icarus was really tall now, and pumping iron to build up his biceps, triceps, pecs, and delts, because he would have to flap his arms so much when he and Daedalus took flight. They'd go up into the sky and away from Minos. The whole adventure of plotting the escape was great fun, and because she and Icarus were doing it together they hardly had time to mope. They had even—"You mustn't tell *anyone*, Asterion, please promise?"—begun a secret worship of her grandsire, Helios, so that Icarus and Daedalus would have safe transit across the heavens. Didn't I recognize the golden gleam in her eye?

I did; and I silently wondered if Daedalus's indulgence toward this golden-haired girl-woman owed anything to her resemblance to Pasiphaë, whose eye was supposed to have held the same gleam. Daedalus had made a device that turned a woman into a cow; now he would turn his son into a bird. Phaedra prattled on about Daedalus and Icarus flying to Sicily, where they would be welcomed and given good things. When she was older, Icarus—a great prince by then—would return to Crete and ask Minos for her hand in marriage.

"How do you know that this will come to pass?"

"Because we love one another and it's a really good plan."

"I hope your dreams will prevail, Phaedra, but then at one time we all hoped that Androgeos would return to Crete in triumph."

"Stuff happens," Phaedra explained, with the conviction of the young that they know the workings of the world. "But you have to hope for the good things, or there won't be any chance of them coming true. I mean, if all the time you think about the bad stuff, there's no room in your head for the good—y'know?"

I had no answer for her sunny suggestion.

Nine

The eleventh group of sacrifices set me off. I don't know why; but the initial bloodletting turned into a rampage instead of what I'd planned, a series of methodical entrapments and executions. Maybe I was too eager to set a record, five murders at a time. We serial killers are constantly inventing new thresholds to cross, new challenges to our ingenuity and mastery lest we become depressed. And we are easily depressed.

Well actually, the *number* of dead wasn't the problem, it was the ratio of men to women victims. In my frenzy I made the mistake of killing five males, resulting in a severe distaff imbalance. For a while it played in my favor. Females being more reluctant to attack than males and more willing to try something new in coupling, in the midst of a harem I felt more at ease than ever, my captives' bosoms, gently flowing hair, and sweet emanations pillowing the hard edges of the labyrinth. And as eaters they were less picky and did not cavil at cannibalism. Perhaps their knowledge that the refrigerator was fully packed emboldened them, for the female majority edged toward revolt. I decided to lay back and see where it took us.

A leader soon emerged: Euadne of Eolis, a beauty with angular lines who was terrific at making gestures that were so imperious, and sighs of boredom that were so impenetrable they would have chilled anyone's blood. Her lackey Podarces—you could hardly call him her second-in-command—sang well, but his beefed up musculature did not offset his deficit in brains. The other male, Inarchus, said little and did less. What followers! The women ruled, but their initial set of decisions was on trivial subjects such as who would tidy up the abattoir of Three Basins, and who on any given day would get to wear the queenly jewels from Pasiphae's tomb. I cheered, however—to myself, of course—when the gals took upon themselves to make the very decision I'd always found the most odious: identifying who should be the next to die and thereby provide the rest of us with food. Talk about your vicious bitches! Euadne's executive council decreed that the next sacrifice must be a female, since the killing of an additional male would unduly burden the remaining one, who would then be forced to service too many sexually avid young women. And then they did the job without me! The victim never saw it coming. She was asleep when they smashed her skull. Euadne's credibility with the remaining captives rose further when the next victim was also female; only later did I realize that this particular girl had once seduced Podarces. Oh, those hidden agendas!

Under distaff dominance, sexual access was available for all, and the pace of the joinings was less hurried, seductions frequently lasting from dawn until dusk, with hands and tongues gradually sliding toward points of stimulation until the anticipation of ecstasy was near unbearable. Between sexual bouts, cleansing and repair of the labyrinth was carried out with a minimum of complaints about drudgery. These women understood the value of an orderly home!

And of art. Should one of us be moved to strew color and line upon the walls of an out-of-the-way chamber, using old powders, wood reduced to charcoal, or a paste of crushed insects, that was condoned, even fostered. Charis wall-painted, Temarca danced, others made rhythms from the ollas, and Inarchus was regularly able to spout humorous observations. Several maidens began to sing an old hymn to the Goddess of No Name; I contributed my bass rendition.

It was just after that concert, as we all lay on our backs in the Vaulted Arena, roaming our eyes over the high ceiling with its filigreed cracks that admitted soft rays of sunlight in which motes of dust floated and pranced, that I started to cry. I don't know why. And no one asked. Rather, my companions began to pat and stroke me, their caresses accompanied by sounds of sympathy that made me cry all the harder out of gratitude for their understanding; this, in turn, spurred them to more specific manipulation. Sensitive scratches on my withers where I could not reach, deep massaging to banish the aches on my gnarled hands and feet, grooming of my tail, erotic brushing of lips and fingertips and vulvas and nipples and beards against my sides and flanks: I began to feel I was a god whose body was being adored by acolytes. I floated in delicate suspension between wakeful clarity and that removal from reality that thrills us in dreams. Transported by caresses, I was open. Pure. Fulfilled. Safe from harm. Aware that these humans could easily hurt me, I knew they would not do so. I blessed my lovers by showering them with a warm spasm and passed over into the most satisfying and contented sleep that ever I experienced in the Middle Realm.

This house of no bedrooms became a vast boudoir. One of us could not pass another in a corridor without an exploratory caress or an invitation to adventure. Sexual hunger exuded from us like sweat from a brow; the more we wiped it away, the more it emerged. From languor and daylong seductions we would shift to rapid, rough encounters whose intensity was heightened by anonymity and darkness. Females found themselves in a state of continual vaginal moistness, male penile shafts were never fully at rest. Attending to naught but desire, we discovered it everywhere and all the time.

Then one day, it stopped for me. When I encountered two or more females together and made sexual overtures, my invitations were greeted with a querulous look, as if I'd made a dismissible joke or a malodorous fart. When I chanced upon Charis or Temarca in a corridor, isolated from the eyes, ears, and noses of the rest of the gang, the young lady would readily assent to a tumbling, but would beg me to keep quiet during our fun and to promise not to later recount the adventure to others. I responded by stimulating her so much that she had no choice but to emit an easily-heard noise.

Everything about Charis of Samos was long—her legs, her arms, the bones of her feet, the eyelashes that hooded her hazel eyes, even her dark nipples. Shortly after she and I had joined on the stairs of the Rogalhida, I found her in the Vaulted Arena, hunched over, knees to chest, eyes brimming with tears.

"Have the other women chastised you for dallying with me?"

She turned her face from me but did not stop sniffling. Suspecting what was happening, I tested my supposition. Going to the Lionhead for water, I surprised there Euadne and Temarca. At my approach they stopped chatting. I flicked my tail at Temarca's rump, as I knew that she preferred rear entry. Glancing furtively at Euadne, she pleaded with me for forbearance because it was "that time of the month."

"Cramps, tiredness, headaches, chores to do, not being in the mood," I ticked off the usual list. "My nose discerns no menstrual flow from you, Temarca. Just this once I'll accept your excuse as a polite way of covering your refusal. In the future, I will demand truth of you—of both of you—as I demand it of myself and of everyone in this prison."

A meeting was called of everyone, in the Vaulted Arena at dusk. "You said that after the initial unpleasantness we'd be equals here, Asterion," Euadne began. "Well, then: As equals we've been choosing what we want to do, and I'm sure you'll agree that the last month has been wondrous for us all, has it not?"

"For the most part."

"If we can each do what we please, and if it pleases each of us humans now to pair off with those more similar to us, is that not our privilege?"

"The privilege of each is not the obligation of all."

"Perhaps everyone likes this arrangement."

"And perhaps they don't, Euadne."

"Let's take a vote," she said, waving her hand aloft. "All those who do like it this way, raise up and say 'aye.'"

The human males as well as the females in the Vaulted Arena said "aye" and put up their hands, even Charis, whose pleasure had echoed so loudly. Had nothing more been said, I might have lived with this condemnatory verdict, perhaps slunk away to brood on my bestial nature. But Euadne could not resist asking, "Are you not going to vote, Asterion?"

"Here's my vote," I said, and with a sudden lunge pierced Podarces' gut with my horn, then rammed him against a solid pillar. The lapdog expired in a mess of blood and sinew, and to the accompaniment of the others' stark screams. Most of them leapt toward the exits.

"The 'nays' have it!"

Charis remained where she was, transfixed, and I hastened to the chase of the others. As I tracked them through the corridors, the scents and spoors that in recent months had faded became once more searingly obvious. My every intuition was genius, my every move inevitable.

"How did you find me?" squealed Hyrnetho when I pulled her from behind the false front of The Eyebrow.

"I smelled your childhood."

"How could you know?" Creusa winced as I dragged her from concealment in the Eighty-First, where she had tried to trick me into the lower labyrinth by propping open the Mirrorgate.

"Last year I ate your sister's brain."

"I hate you," snarled Euadne, small daggers in hand, when as I located her and Inarchus on either end of the Two Entwined Snakes galleries. I let them draw blood, then herded them too back to the Vaulted Arena.

Temarca sat, docile, next to a stanchion, while Charis shivered in a corner, eyes wide and wildly roaming, her long arms clamped tight about her knees. Ignoring Charis for the moment, I commanded the others to convey Podarces' body to Three Basins for storage while Temarca cleaned up the mess at his death site.

Charis's shock was very deep. I was afraid that unless she

was relieved of it she would sit in her hunched position until she died.

When all the others had returned from their chore, I addressed them formally. "Many things that happen in this Middle Realm result from the gods tracing their designs upon the walls of our lives. We may not be able to understand the designs, but we can live in harmony with them. The gods now lift from you, Charis, the burden of choosing to live or not. Responsibility for that now lodges in me. I impose order, I am your terror and your salvation. Henceforth you will always have a purpose for I will give it to you, speaking at times from my mouth, then again from the walls, and most often from within your own brain. Spend the day stimulating yourself, or painting the walls, or screaming until exhausted, or simply sleeping—whatever—for from now on you are completely free."

When Charis fixed her hazel eyes on me, smiled, and rose to assist Temarca in cleaning, I knew I had helped her.

The inability of the others to do anything but take orders encouraged me to make real my every blood fantasy. My instructions intensified: Flagellate one another to bright pinnacles of pain, lap the seeping, intoxicating blood and draw with it upon the walls the designs of Poseidon. Urgently now, the demands spewed from me: Never walk but run; never speak but shout; know tenderness only as the absence of pain. We must live at fever pitch. We must raise the dead from Three Basins and dance with them. We must ingest their putrefying flesh, then vomit and starve ourselves until our howling disturbs the moon and causes the female acolytes to devour alive Inarchus, the remaining captive who dares to be male.

I awoke, alone, in an inner chamber. How much time had passed? Were any of the captives alive? In hiding? A cursory tour of the upper galleries revealed, to my mounting dismay, a finger here, a leg there, a half-gnawed bone further on, dried blood smeared upon walls and, in Three Basins, several sundered bodies. Canopic jars were stuffed with organs and entrails so putrid that no amount of sluicing water would entirely dissipate the stench. The most distressing aspect of the carnage was my inability to remember these killings. From the evidence of the savagery I had doubtless participated, but had I done so alone? I simply did not know.

I found three women, alive, in the chamber of the Two Entwined Snakes. Euadne's anger now expressed itself in continual self-flagellation. Temarca was unmoving; she stirred only if I specifically directed her: Eat this, move your left hand up and around the cup thusly, crouch to defecate in that jar. Only Charis seemed free, swaying to an inner music, tracing her fingers and toes on the walls, all the while smiling tenderly. The three were present but not present, and none of them could vouchsafe me any information about the time that we must have jointly spent in torture, murder, and cannibalism.

I had failed, failed at life's fundamental task, to be acutely aware of the world and of oneself in it. Often, such ignorance is invisible to us, and we only realize its absence much later. In this instance it was immediately and blindingly obvious to me: Because I had been insufficiently aware, terrible things had happened. Not the killings themselves—they were awful, but I'd killed many times before. Rather, what was awful was that I had incited other human beings to murder, and beyond murder, to wanton savagery. In doing so, I had presumptuously taken upon myself the prerogatives of a god.

Had I wanted to do that? Yes, I decided, and out of a desire to reach the soaring, confident consciousness that I associated with godhead, a transcendent, creative excitement in which nothing was forbidden. But having reached godhead, what had ensued? What had this particular god wrought? Damage! Awful damage! Not awe-some but aw-ful.

How disgusting of me.

In anguish at what had occurred—at what I had done—I became repentant. In the moons that followed I tried to make up for my bad deeds. I devoted myself to ministering to my three mad acolytes, Euadne, Temarca, and Charis, feeding them morsels of Meat and cups of water, cleansing them when they soiled themselves, calming their intense fright. But as I gazed at their tormented, sleeping forms in the crepuscular gloom I could not prevent lust mixing with my compassion. I barely managed to hold lust in check. I was more of a monster than I had ever allowed myself to understand.

Temarca's retreat into immobility became more and more complete. From having to instruct her to eat, I was forced to descend to telling her to chew, then to ordering her to swallow, and then to pleading with her stomach to digest the food. Though I commanded her heart to beat and her lungs to breathe and her entrails to process her wastes, when my voice hoarsened from constant pleading, I lost her. By morning she was beyond response.

I took away Euadne's instruments of flagellation, but she used the length of a gallery to build up a running start and slam herself against the walls, I transferred her to a smaller cubicle, where I was soon forced to cut her fingernails so she could not tear at herself. But I could not prevent her from crawling inside an olla and choking on the desiccant powder the priestesses had used to preserve the dead.

After these two bitter deaths I led my lone mad Charis deeper into the labyrinth, through the Eighty-First Chamber and its Mirrorgate, down along the ossuary to the magnificence of Pasiphae's crypt. Throughout the other sacrifices' terrible last days and nights, Charis had grown stronger in body and more carefree and supple in her dances and designs. The raiments of a queen and the evocative, painted descriptions of Pasiphae's life somehow made Charis feel more at one with her fantasies. Indeed, in these surroundings she seemed happy, caressing me on one of her endless whirls, directing her fingers and their colors to the unadorned ninth panel of the high, vaulted space.

"Pasiphaë was pregnant with Asterion," Charis sang tunelessly.

"Yes," I answered. "She was pregnant with Asterion."

"And so am I."

Ten

Humanity shares with the gods an inability to see the exact contours of the future, even when all the signs point to what it will be.

My future shouted at me in two shapes: that of Charis's rapidly-extending belly, and that of the black-sailed toy boat billowing with the inner wind of the floor of the Cone of the Disappearing Ceiling. Daedalus had sent this mini-vessel to me as thanks for my forwarding of feathers, but surely also as a warning of what lay ahead. He was being specific, but I had no idea of that. He presumed that I would know that only the Athenians, of all the seafarers, had the effrontery to roam the briny with their sails dyed black. This was common knowledge to the islanders, but since I only knew what filtered through to me from my captives, his presumption was in error, for none had ever told me about the black sails. So what I "got" from the toy was a general warning about danger coming from the next group of sacrifices.

In any event, the color of the black sails matched my mood. While I was intoxicated by the possibility of an heir to my kingdom now in Charis's belly, I crumpled beneath the balancing need to spare that offspring the pain of life as a monster. I thought about killing Charis and the passenger in her womb. But I balked at doing so—what right had I to cut off my potential offspring's possibilities of transfiguration, of reaching beyond its probable physical manifestation?

As I mulled over these thoughts in the Lionhead Basin, to which I transferred the black-sailed toy ship, I was interrupted by a jumble of palace-related noises that became audible even in a chamber that was not directly connected to the palace. To hear it better, I hastened to the Cone of the Disappearing Ceiling.

The hue and cry coming from that funnel was of the sort that usually preceded the arrival of sacrifices. This batch was ahead of schedule. I couldn't waste time figuring out why, because the sounds suggested they would shortly be forced into the labyrinth, where Charis and I would have to deal with them.

They might kill Charis! That I could not allow.

I coaxed my mad love into Three Basins, near the cached Meat and water supply. The cubicle's existence would be difficult for neophytes to infer, and its narrow entrance could be easily defended. Thus did Charis and her belly become my secret, the private core of my labyrinth. In this charnel house of a maze, I hid life incipient.

I prowled the upper galleries. What was delaying the captives? Had Minos invented new humiliations for them? My hunger throbbed. Try as I might to prevent the sensations, my mouth salivated, my heart pounded. I moaned in expectation, and when the victims did not appear my moans morphed into roars, roars that I told myself were practice for scaring the captives. If I could frighten them into compliance I might not have to kill them all right away. Just one. Or two. I looked forward to a really satisfying rip of my jaws through solid, fresh Meat. Faint screams from the palace meshed with my roars and further intermingled with a timorous trembling of the earth. Did my roars anticipate or reflect these tremors? I tested my lungs with roars until the entire labyrinth reverberated with my noise. The echoes faded to cracking sounds, which I sensed were coming from the Vaulted Arena; trotting there, I found new fissures in the already-compromised ceiling. I hurried back to the Cone of the Disappearing Ceiling, and there became privy to a sound I had thought I might never again hear, the scrape and whine of the descending scarlet-rope apparatus.

Ariadne was garbed in the white, head-to-toe robe of a priestess, but it was parted to display her lovely breasts, the nipples tinted to the dark color of her hair and scented to draw the nose as well as the eyes. Having by now had more experience of women, I was able to appreciate that this twenty-year-old gliding to rest in front of me was at the peak of youthful beauty. Her body might later ripen to more lush proportions, her mind blossom with mature womanly wit, but here before me was maidenly perfection. I was glad I had a secret hidden away in the folds of the labyrinth, a counterpoint to the power that Ariadne had always exerted upon me. She passed over a hand-basket containing foods I had not enjoyed since entering the labyrinth, dressed chicken, fish, a half-dozen prepared vegetables, and a variety of cakes. As I gulped everything down, Ariadne said, "The moment has come, Asterion. What we've been waiting for all these years."

"Has Minos decided to abdicate?"

"Of course not. But there's an opportunity to take the kingdom from him."

"By magic?" The turtledove wings were really excellent.

"Why are you so contrary today, Asterion? This is a crucial time, and you must listen to me. And help me."

"You never visit without a purpose, my sister."

Ariadne ignored the reproach. "The man who will overthrow the evil empire is here, and we must do everything we can to help him."

"Who is this amazing guy?"

"Theseus, son of Aegeus and prince of Athens."

The name, the title, the provenance rang in my ears; and I understood from Ariadne's behavior that they did more than echo in hers. "Why should I help him?"

"Because he is sacred to Poseidon," Ariadne said with reverence, and proceeded to relate the tale of his arrival in the harbor.

When the black-sailed craft had entered the port, with its youths and maidens destined for the labyrinth, Theseus was among them and announced himself as the son of Aegeus. For Athens to have sent such a prestigious sacrifice was deemed by the guards to be of interest to Minos, so they alerted the palace.

The king traveled to the port, accompanied by Ariadne, Phaedra, and a large retinue to welcome the sacrifices. Once Minos was in hearing distance, Theseus boasted of his own closeness to Poseidon. Minos scoffed. Theseus offered to provide proof.

Irony is of the essence to the human condition: Here was Theseus, seeking to prove his nearness to the god Poseidon to Minos, whose own connection to Poseidon had once been undeniably demonstrated by the appearance and actions of the white bull.

With deepening despair I heard from Ariadne how Minos had taken Theseus's bait. At the Athenian's request, Ariadne had thrown into the waters a queenly ring.

"One that belonged to Pasiphaë?"

"Yes. How did you guess?"

"It's what I would have done. On with your tale."

According to Ariadne, Prince Theseus prayed aloud to Poseidon to have the ring brought to him from the depths. Moments later, a dolphin surfaced with the bauble in its jaws and deposited it in Theseus's outstretched hand. The prince then returned the family jewel to Ariadne. Minos laughed, allowed that he was impressed, and said that the reward for Theseus's magic would be a sumptuous meal at the royal table—his last, before being given to Asterion, who would quickly introduce Theseus to the Netherworld, where Theseus might take up with Poseidon the entire matter of his visit to Crete. All fourteen Athenians were then clapped in shackles.

"At dinner I sat next to Theseus and we became better acquainted."

"Is Theseus your new lover?"

"No, Asterion."

"But you wish him to be."

"I have pledged myself to him—in exchange for his doing something for us."

"Bring down Minos's empire? Has Daedalus taught you nothing? How can you be so blind? If Minos should fall, Theseus will take you as booty even if you decide you don't want to go.

Faugh! Compulsion disguised as love! Will you humans never learn to reason properly?"

"The plan can succeed, Asterion. Theseus and his comrades will enter the labyrinth, but you must let them live—work with them to destroy the labyrinth, so we can all be free."

"Whatever 'being free' means."

"Free to live as we hoped we would, Asterion."

"And how will Theseus contrive to wreck the labyrinth and then to escape it? What, specifically, will he do that others before him have failed to do?"

"He won't reveal his plan to me, because he says that whoever knows it might be compromised. He says I must trust him."

"Trust is a much overrated emotional coin, and far too human a bulwark for any serious endeavor. Am I to sit on my haunches and trust the Athenian prince to do what he says he will do?"

"As I've told you before, Asterion, you do not know your own strength. You must join with Theseus to summon Poseidon, who will bring down everything."

Ariadne was correct to discern that my kinship with the god of tremors and waves had been growing, and that I now understood it might well be possible for me to summon Poseidon's wrath—but the whole plan depended too much on Poseidon's willingness to tear down the twin institutional seats of Minos's empire, the palace and the labyrinth; and in the midst of that destruction to distinguish good from bad, and to punish the multitude while protecting a few from harm.

"What has Daedalus to say about this?"

"Daedalus and Icarus will use the confusion to fly away. Their wings are prepared and the catapult is already strung."

"And who will cut the catapult's cord when the moment comes?"

"Phaedra, of course. She'd do anything for Icarus."

Ariadne beseeched me to conduct Theseus and his companions through the labyrinth to this very spot, the Cone of the Disappearing Ceiling. She would then descend again in the rope basket to meet them, and assist us all in our escape.

"That basket has always been too frail to accept my bulk."

"Daedalus has made it stronger," Ariadne insisted, and I saw now that the conveyance had indeed been widened, deepened, and reinforced. She spoke of the old priestesses who would haul up the Athenians and even bring up the Minotaur, that nice old monster who had so courageously guarded their sacred temple during the dark years of Minoan era.

I revised my estimate. All aspects of the scheme that did not directly depend upon divine cooperation had been carefully considered. Theseus was quite the strategist, and Ariadne, or perhaps Daedalus, had added a few splendid tweaks to the plan. It could work! And I was pleased that the priestesses would finally acknowledge how hard I had worked to preserve the special character of their sanctuary.

Down here in Hades' Hostel, in trying to comprehend how after years in the labyrinth I could have allowed myself to be so easily led to slaughter, I see that the most crucial flattery was Ariadne's last, the priestesses' compliment to me for preserving the labyrinth. They would appreciate *me*? Me, the Minotaur? Me the epitome of male rapaciousness? Me, the usurper of the domain of the Goddess With No Name? Me, who had enabled Minos to take over their temple and defile it? Ariadne had certainly slung her hobble at exactly the right spot—my pride— and just at the very moment when I should have more carefully questioned the arrangements. Why was there any need for a scarlet-rope exit from the labyrinth if the plan was to destroy the labyrinth? Why destroy the labyrinth if the plan was to restore the priestesses to their domain? I asked neither of these questions, nor any of the others that might have been relevant.

Only later did I realize a basic truth: that giving one's trust does not eliminate one's capacity to reason, it bypasses that capacity entirely. I asked of Ariadne only that as a sign of good will she vouchsafe me a kiss.

"On the lips?"

"Yes. I see that you tremble. Is it with disgust or desire, my sister?"

"'Twas ever both," she responded, and flowed into my arms as if she had always been my lover and was returning to me after a momentary hiatus in our entwining. Passionate and fierce, her kiss was acknowledgment that I had troubled her sleep as often as she had haunted mine.

Such a female whirlwind of lust and benevolence was too good for Theseus.

My fellow dwellers in the House of Hades, although you have only been in residence for a short spell, I'm certain that one of your pleasures has been to realize, as I did upon my arrival long ago, that death is not so terrible. To the living, of course, death seems so absolute that it is blown all out of proportion; the living lose sight of death as a transformative event, one that of course has an enormous impact on one's life, but no more so than one's birth, a huge event over which we have even less control.

I knew that something exciting was in the works when on a cloudless, sun-drenched day crowds began to gather on the cliffs above the Navel and at the outer rim of the Gallery of the Thirteen Portals. The watchers raucously called upon me to wreak vengeance upon the Athenians who were approaching my labyrinth.

Despite my promise to Ariadne of forbearance to the captives, I had half a mind to oblige the crowd by killing a few of the Athenians as soon as they entered my domain. To cool down, I went to do a last-moment check on Charis, and discovered that her birthing pangs had begun, that our offspring was about to be born. A child! Of mine! I tried to help her, but she kept telling me that there was nothing I could do, and shooed me away. Noises were coming from the Gallery of Thirteen

Portals. By the time I returned there, the captives had already been shoved inside the labyrinth and the entrance had been re-sealed behind them.

As the captives caught sight of me they screamed, a noise greeted with cheers by the outside crowd.

"Keep yelling," I advised the captives in a moderate voice. "Let them out there think that I frighten you."

"Great Apollo," said one of them. "It speaks!"

These Athenians were more vigorously athletic than they were beautiful, and they were also smart, evidenced by their sticking together in a phalanx, as though to counter my usual tactic of separating out individuals so I could make easy kills and achieve dominance. These were thirteen highly trained and disciplined men and women. Thirteen? Why were they not fourteen?

"Which of you is Theseus?"

"I am," said one man.

"So am I," echoed another.

"Theseus is my name," countered one woman.

"So be it," I exclaimed, throwing aloft my cloven hands and flicking my tail in exasperation. "On with the show. We must demonstrate to those on the outside that I, the Minotaur, am making their sacrifices. Once we've done that, they'll be satisfied and will return home. So I'm going to grab you, young lady Theseus, right in front of the wall. The rest of you, make appro-priately frightened noises, and follow me."

Before the captives could protest I swept up the young woman, tucked her under my arm, and loped along the trans-lucent wall in such a way as to make sure that our joint outline was clearly visible to the watchers. A welcoming roar greeted my demonstration. My prize was light as a feather, a succulent mor-sel. I fancied taking a bite of her pretty buttocks, then dangling near my jaws, but contented myself with a rough nuzzle. That provoked a terrified scream and a most unladylike loosening of the bowels. Her haunch became less appealing.

I reached through to the Vaulted Arena and there politely

dumped my burden. Unharmed, she was surrounded and comforted by her mates. I lit a single torch and invited the group to follow me further into the labyrinth, informing them that we would soon reach the meeting place designated by Ariadne. They came along willingly, now understanding the charade that I had been playing out. They helped me enact another scene of that charade near the Navel, above which a second sector of the crowd awaited: from an antechamber that could not be seen from above, I threw out into the little garden a half-gnawed head of a victim from an earlier cycle, and they accompanied it by screams and shrieks. The sight produced answering huzzahs from the watchers above, on the lips of the canyon.

As I bowed to my new captives, who applauded me silently for the charade, it dawned on me that all of the schemes I had evolved during my long confinement in the labyrinth were now bearing fruit, in the sense of their furthering the cause of the captives' and my deliverance. I allowed myself some self-congratulatory thoughts about the great role I was playing in the immensely important task of overthrowing Minos and his savage empire.

As I guided the captives through the labyrinth, the glare of my torch revealed the corridors as especially beautiful. By moving the torch this way and that I directed my guests' eyes to the notable architectural and decorative features. So impressed were the gawkers that I considered taking detours to afford them a better sense of the temple's magnificence, but stifled the impulse to more quickly reach the appointed meeting place, the Chamber of the Disappearing Ceiling.

In that large, circular chamber the thirteen Athenians and I all gazed expectantly aloft, trying to discern what was far above and shrouded in darkness. Why were there not fourteen captives? I still did not know. The plan was for Ariadne to meet Theseus here. Although the chamber was spacious, it had only two entrances, and I noticed that the group clustered near these, a quite understandable activity in such a strange place.

Charis's birthing chamber was not far from this one, and I

slipped out to go there and check on the progress of her labor. She was still in the grip of pain, unable as yet to push out her burden. I wanted to stay but heard the grinding noise of the apparatus in the Cone of the Disappearing Ceiling and left her to return to that chamber. A figure was descending toward us. In the upper limit of the torchlight I caught sight of the white robe and sandals, and my nose was overwhelmed with the familiar intoxicants of Ariadne's lavender and sandalwood. She bore some sort of treasure, equally muffled in white cloth. I peered through the gloom in hope of glimpsing the mood on my sister's face, but it remained shadowed by her robe, and I could see only her remarkable black hair, that silken dark crown. The Athenians pressed with me toward the center of the floor, where the conveyance would land. As it touched down, the still-hooded figure stepped out and moved aside. The Athenians rushed for the basket and its cloth-covered contents.

The white-robed, black-haired, lavender-scented creature turned to face me—and it had a double-edged labrys in its hands and it was not Ariadne but a beardless, muscular, cross-dressing young man who swung that axe at me, forcing me to jump back! Out of the corner of my eye I saw that the Athenians had also filled their hands with double-axes and were advancing on me in a closing circle.

The false female was the true Theseus! Ariadne must have hidden him in her chamber. The plan to demolish Minos's empire meant, first off, killing the Minotaur! My betrayal was absolute. I knew also that it was not Theseus or Minos who betrayed me: My betrayer was my sister, to whom I had ever abandoned my reason.

I was the Minotaur still, and they would not so easily carve me up! I dashed out of the chamber and ran through the labyrinth. They pursued me, torches and axes to the fore. In an outer corridor of the Onion I charged a gap between axe-wielders, dispatching two but receiving in return deep slashes to my withers. These blows brought me to my knees in pain. From the depths of my betrayed being, then, I uttered a roar—the loudest, greatest, most anguished roar I had ever made, the roar I had always known I was capable of making, the ultimate bellow of despair, a noise lamenting how love had been turned against me, a noise expressing my desire that as I perished the world would die with me.

Rumbling and tremors began. I limped quickly onward to the birthing chamber. Entering, I found Charis even more in extremis. I would defend her, defend the offspring of mine that was being born. Did I see the crown of a head between her thighs? As I looked, the blows of my pursuers continued to cut me. Head. Neck. Back. Thighs.

I roared in supplication to father Poseidon to avenge me on every perfidious human on the island of Crete. Instanter, the labyrinth began shaking. There was the hideous high screech of rock against rock, the pounding guttural growl of water overwhelming its boundaries. The ceiling cracked. Pieces of it fell—or was that my blood cascading down into my eyes, negating my vision? Fissures appeared in the floor beneath me—or were they the wounds that the repeated blows opened in my outstretched limbs? Strength resided now only in my voice.

Bring it all down, Poseidon, they must die as I die! Punish them for their cowardice and deception and blasphemy in killing your creature!

The confusion, the shaking, and the upheaval deflected the labrys-swings. One Athenian chopped through another: A moment of respite and triumph. I leaned into the whirlwind of pain. Blood spurted out of me with astonishing force, emptying from myriad wounds, thickening my tongue, flooding my brain. The labyrinth and I would be destroyed together!

Death and birth approached simultaneously.

Like my half-brother Polyphemus, I could no longer see, but I heard Theseus cry for one last blow, and for everyone else to go to the ropes to escape the crashing universe. Then I could not hear or smell or see, but nonetheless sensed Theseus standing over me, his betrayal-honed labrys raised high. I screamed to Poseidon to curse the race of humans for their presumptuous claim to an existence whose sweetness they never appreciated. The weapon descended toward my neck, I felt the knife-edge bite in and almost through, felt life accelerate away from me like a shooting star.

Eleven

Hermes of the winged sandals commanded me to follow his heels. Unable to resist, I rose from the bloody labyrinth floor and flowed with the messenger god. I knew I was dead but I was still me! Although suffused with sadness I also felt the urge to laugh, believing that the rigor of my prior days in the Middle Realm had singularly prepared me for the torture gauntlet of the afterlife.

Leaving behind land, then sea, and then sky, we coursed on into unrelenting vastness. How inconsequential in the universe is man and all his works! I saw the titan Atlas, his muscles and back straining with the weight of the intersection of earth and sky, the nymphs Night and Day endlessly chasing one another at his feet. Beyond Atlas were gates crawling with fantastic figures, gates that opened at our approach to reveal an amorphous, spongy landmass wreathed in rivers and illumined only by the inner fires whose noxious smoke masked its edges.

As you recently dead no doubt did, I felt that I was somewhere beyond—not above nor below but in a different spatial relation to the Middle Realm. Only the complete absence of sunlight made me think that this was Netherworld.

Hermes deposited me at the ferry dock on the shores of the Styx. Those fully human beings who arrived at the same moment were tossed into the seething, foul-smelling Styx; they screamed in terror until the liquid rendered them dumb and speechless, a condition in which, I learned, they would remain for a year. I had no coin for ferryman Charon to take me across the Styx, but in his purse were many coins stamped with my likeness; after comparing me to those miniature Minotaurs, he readily poled me to the far shore. There, though I had naught in my pockets to feed Cerberus's three dog heads, the hellhound was so astonished to see a demi-bull in the region reserved for the harrowing of humans that he too allowed me to pass. The ferry brought me to what seemed to be solid land but was the banks of a second river, the Cocytus, River of Lamentation. On that spit of solidity between the Styx and the Cocytus the unconsecrated must roam for a hundred years before transitioning further into the afterlife.

I had certainly not been consecrated, not even formally buried, but the collapse of the labyrinth and palace on top of me was evidently considered adequate entombment, so I was spared a century of Cocytean exile. But my ability to wander, indeed all of my movement, was restricted, nay, controlled by the halvoids that seemed able to conduct me hither and yon, and that I had no power to resist. These half-sized things had humanoid bodies, trunks, arms, and legs but no heads, in order that they not be mistaken for graven images of gods or men.

They most resembled the toys made by Daedalus to amuse the children in the palace at Knossos, and at first I smiled at them, until they surrounded me and I discovered that in their presence I had no volition. That overwhelmed me with dread. They took me on a sightseeing tour, the horrors of which were almost unimaginable. Those of you who have not been so royally treated should consider yourselves fortunate.

Or would you rather that the halvoids toss you into the Phlegethon, River of Liquid Fire, where your past sins would be leached out in much the same way that metallic ore is scorched in fire to burn away impurities? How about if they forced you to do a stint on the bare hills above the Phlegethon, where tens of thousands of the dead from recent wars move about, their tears cumulating into the Cocytus? Or perhaps you'd prefer to be dipped in the Acheron, downstream where the Phlegethon and the Cocytus merge? The Acheron is the place chosen to harrow the billions who have succumbed to disease. Malaria, dengue, cancer, typhoid, dysentery. Did you think that because you simply contracted something fatal and died, and had done nothing to cause your own death, that you would escape Hell? The gods hold us responsible for everything.

I had to admire the set-up in Netherworld. The Hadean desert is carved up into island-plains by eight inner coils of the Styx. Each solid land between the coils is occupied by a different set of harrowers and harrowed. Over there is the real murderers row, where killers are assaulted by their victims. You don't qualify for that? How about for the one where parents are flagellated by the children they abused? My favorite is the third, where suicides pillory their former families, lovers, and neighbors, for prior maltreatment. Down here we're big on responsibility.

Toward the interior of the desert, the terrain begins to slope downward. You new shades can't see the end point from here, but let me assure you that although at first the incline is only modest, the angle then steepens and eventually you lose your footing and are cascaded into the center of a whirlpool of sand and rock, and then through that into interminable space, where you fall, fall, and keep falling until you enter a region of gyrating, stinging ice crystals. That is Tartarus's bailiwick, the intense punishment area of the gods. You ordinary humans are routinely spared entry therein. For me to view it, supposedly as a tourist with halvoid guides, was a privilege I would have been happy to forego.

Before me in the hurtful Tartaran mist loomed three awful, amorphous, gray malevolences, the Furies, created by Cronos from the bloody droppings of his castrated sire Uranus. Tisiphone, Megaera, and Allecto wear cowls that frame their bloodshot eyes; each holds in one claw a white-hot torch and in the other a scourge of fanged, living serpents. The Furies are pure revenge, and they hate demi-gods more than they hate humans. Chief among their targets for flagellation are those god-begotten from whom the gods have removed their divine protection. Well, my god had certainly forsaken me, so I was definitely in that group! My fright increased when I caught sight of hapless

Ixion, who had done nothing more than boast of being the lover of the goddess Hera. Ixion was strapped to a ceaselessly turning wheel that dipped him into and out of a cauldron of molten metal. I also saw there the shadow of Sisyphus, who in the Middle Realm had been far too cunning and here eternally struggled with his boulder toward the top of the vortex, whence it toppled him again into the abyss.

A third beam of light caught a half-man, half-bird creature, evidently a recent arrival, as it was being whirled down at us by another set of halvoids. The hag trio of Furies seized on this creature, trussed him upon a spit and fixed it in the swirling void so that its back was ever seared by the same furnace that afflicted Ixion, while his front was simultaneously chilled by the frigid ice crystals. The creature was human-like and familiar, and soon I recognized that under the feathers was the blonde adolescent human physique of Icarus. Even though I hadn't seen him in many a year, he still resembled the tyke that had once roamed the Minoan palace with Phaedra. In the grasp of Tartarus, Icky writhed in pain, his heated side craving the cool, his near-frozen side craving the warmth; neither side could reach relief.

Conflicting emotions tore at me. The presence of Icarus here meant that my sister Phaedra must be distraught, but since Icarus's father, Daedalus, was not here, that meant that my friend was still alive. But why subject Daedalus's poor sweet son to such painful torment? And why was I not pilloried next to him?

The halvoids collected me from Tartarus's bailiwick and then conducted me across the fire-and-tear-scarred plain to a grove of delicately-leaved acacia trees, an incongruous sight in this wasteland. Within the grove were two marble thrones. One was topped by a single flame that emanated from no visible source and consumed no fuel. The other was empty of light.

"So you are the Minotaur," intoned a voice from the flame.

At the sound of the voice I felt forced to my knees. Although I no longer had a body, bodily sensations afflicted me still.

"I am your uncle, Hades. Do not ask me to remove the helmet of invisibility and prove my existence."

135

I held back such a request, and the flame flickered in amusement.

So this was Hades! The other throne must be for his wife, Persephone, absent on her annual sojourn in the Middle Realm.

"You accomplished much while alive, Asterion—killed many, frightened more, and symbolized the male gods' terrors on earth. But the punishments you offered your captives were rather naïve. Here those are refined. Are you ready to suffer?"

"I have imagined a tree continually seared by hate, throbbing with pain in every branch but not allowed to die."

"A good answer," the flame allowed. "I must tell Tisiphone to add that to her repertoire. Better yet: Enter my service, nephew. I have need for a beast who understands humans."

"What would I do, great lord?"

"Make such trees as you have imagined."

"Humans suffer enough in the Middle Realm."

"Yes, and they will continue to do so whether or not you enter my service. Foster their transformation or share their harrowing. Decide, Asterion."

For me it was a no-brainer.

No sooner had I made up my half-human mind that I had done enough damage to the human race and would do no more, and well before I was able to say so aloud, I was thrown back through the vortex and into the clutches of Tartarus. There, for a period of time whose length I was unable to calculate, I was successively strapped to Ixion's awful wheel, made to push Sisyphus's stone, and pinioned in place of Icarus. While I writhed on various racks, the Furies demonstrated that the mind was their most fertile stomping ground. Tisiphone, Megaera, and Allecto knew my character intimately, as evidenced by the aptness of their torments. At their bidding I retraced every step of my mortal days, and in each I saw my errors and sins. Under the lashes of the Furies I doubted every decision I ever made and every action I ever took in the Middle Realm, until I came to accept that their terrible retribution on me was entirely justified. I had indeed been the cause of all my misery, including my birth.

After my reduction to blubbering impotence, when I was still trapped and pilloried to the rack of my mind, the Furies dangled before me, just out of reach, the glistening bunch of sweet grapes, the cooling rain shower, the enemy I longed to smite, the benevolence of the child's smile. I realized at last that our ultimate agonies are our emotions that cannot be satisfied.

Only when I had reached that nadir was I released from Tartarus's grasp and brought here to this grove that is watered by both Lethe and Mnemosyne, to choose from which stream I would drink. Calm, murmuring Lethe lay before me with her promise of gentle caress, a beautiful mother in whose care all troubles dissolve. Her oblivion did not hold out forgiveness but did offer release from all that I had known in the Middle Realm. To be immersed in Lethe is to be cleansed and made ready for another chance at mortal life, although my future physical shape would not be known to me—or even if, the next time around, I would be human or bovine or something else. And I certainly would not know in advance whether a better or worse fate would await me. The more turbulent Mnemosyne promised the opposite of oblivion, greater awareness, heightened recall of my former life. To quaff of Mnemosyne is to remain in Hades' House, for the gods forbid the carrying of one's memories of a former life into the next. To drink of her, however, holds out the eventual possibility of spiritual transformation, of being granted entry to Elysium, those hillsides of joy beyond the Isles of the Blest: to walk calmly in sunlight through a field of asphodels!

I had not decided which stream to sample when the fully-tortured Icarus appeared at the grove, drank gratefully from Lethe and was relieved of his memories. His rehab was complete. But rather than being given another go-around at human existence in the Middle Realm, he was transformed into a golden-headed vulture. I was told by later arrivals to Hell that although in the air the golden vulture appears beautiful and strong, with immensely wide wings able to soar for hours on the upper air currents, when he alights on land to take his sustenance from carrion, he is surpassingly ugly and ungainly, detested by all mortals.

Icarus's relatively rapid return to the Middle Realm—even in an altered state—was in keeping with the pattern of Hades' domain: infants who die spend only an eye-blink of time here, while men and women who perish in old age reside here quite a while, although the exact length of their purgation varies with the degree of sin in their former lives. I was pleased to note that fast-track treatment had been given to those relatively young victims sacrificed through me. Most of them had already returned to the Middle Realm before I arrived. The remainder were in the cohort of the unjustly murdered and the victims of true accidents, and were well on their way to ultimate reboots; I regretted only their unavailability to hash over old times with me.

Still trying to choose whether my poison was quiet Lethe or turbulent Mnemosyne, I caught sight of a great beauty whose regal bearing was apparent as she entered the grove of cypress and poplar. Though I had never known my mother while she was alive, I recognized Pasiphaë from the likeness in her tomb.

"Hail Pasiphaë, queen of Crete."

"And hello, to you, Asterion. That you have entered Hades' realm attests to your residual humanity—my gift—as well as to the godly rather than the purely animal nature of my inseminator."

My mother and I then traded stories. She filled me in on the details of events that had preceded my birth, up to and including her final years and death.

After Pasiphaë's recitation had ended, I inquired, "You have no regrets?"

"Not in the large matters."

"Perhaps your refusal to atone is what keeps you here."

"No. I am here because I fulfilled my destiny in the Middle Realm, a life of many passions. The gods may control us, Asterion, but they will never understand the true roles of passion in human life. I began by loving the Old Goddess with No Name, and then I loved Minos. Ardently. Enough to desert the old Goddess, enough to bear him eight human children, enough to hurt him grievously when my love was spurned. And then I loved you, Asterion, before you were born, loved you enough to bear you even though I knew that your emergence would cause my death."

"I thank you for allowing me life, even though my days and nights brimmed with bitterness. May I ask another question: Why did you desert the Goddess of No Name?"

"Being in harness to a power you cannot see, hear, or feel is frustrating and boring. Change, movement, danger, commitment even when it hurts: that's what's exciting about life."

"The Goddess's cycles are too predictable?"

"Yes, and she is too unappeasable. Do you defend her, Asterion? You who have done more than anyone to cause her eclipse?"

"I did so not of my own choosing. 'Twas at Minos's behest."

"Have you learned nothing from the Furies, my son? Everything is of our own choosing. In their eyes, I should have known that you would become a monster before I gave in to my urge to mate with the white bull."

"Ridiculous! Even the gods do not know precisely what the future may bring."

"As you are finding out, Asterion, the gods hold us to higher standards than they hold themselves. The Furies accuse me of having Circe curse Minos so I would later betray him with the bull—even that I permitted Minos to deceive me in the first place so that I could then curse him and start the whole bloody cycle of events."

"Then the gods really do not so much hate us as envy us."

"Yes. We humans live, conscious that time is fleeting, and while taking little care to sequester some time for our later use; we give ourselves wholeheartedly to our lovers and to our children and to our work, knowing that our gifts may be unrequited; and then, after having known for most of our lives that our deaths were inevitable, we die. Immortals have no such deep passions, Asterion, they have whims. The gods may be powerful, but human beings are grandly sensate and grandly vulnerable."

She cupped her hands and drank deeply from Mnemosyne. After meeting her, I have done the same.

Twelve

In the Middle Realm, many lies are told about the afterlife. That we will be happier once relieved of mortal pains and cares. That our goodness will suffice us with the gods. That on the other side of death we will joyfully be reunited with previously departed friends and loved ones.

My fellow shades, as you and I have found out, that's baloney. First of all, we suffer in Netherworld, regardless of what we have done or not done in the Middle Realm. Second, the gods are unimpressed by our so-called goodness. And as for rekindling alliances from the Middle Realm, it doesn't happen very often. How could it, since a major part of the all-consuming process of redemption, down here, is accepting responsibility for and punishment of our sins of commission and omission? And since those who punish us, down here, are the relatives and friends against whom we committed most of our sins?

But I was an exception to the guilt-edged third rule. On that darkling plain I did reconnect with my mother, and not long after that chat saw a more familiar shade bathing in the slag of the Phlegethon.

"Daedalus!"

"Asterion! Come on in—the molten lava's fine!"

"No, thanks. Have you been harrowed by Icarus?"

"Icarus? Just a tad. Mostly by Talos."

"The young man you killed in Athens," I recalled.

"My nephew, actually. Creator of the saw and the zipper. He tarried here, awaiting my arrival. And his wrath was justified."

"Tell me of your journey."

141

According to Daedalus, after Phaedra had cut the cord on the catapult and launched him and Icarus into the air, they flew north by northwest over the sea on wings of feathers attached to their arms by beeswax. "I warned Icarus not to swoop too low and risk sopping the wings with water, and not to soar too high and risk the sun melting the wax and causing a fall," Daedalus said. "My mistake, Asterion, was to believe that our progress through the æther was in thrall to Helios, charioteer of the sun, sire of your mother Pasiphaë. I had not reckoned that Helios had been displaced by Apollo, a newer sun god more closely allied with Zeus and his brothers. Nor had I factored in that Apollo was much less benevolent than the deity he supplanted."

In a concatenation of offenses religious, filial, and physiochemical, Icarus did precisely what Daedalus had warned him against doing. Intoxicated by flight, he soared so high that the beeswax melted and parts of his wings dropped off, causing him to swiftly plummet into the bosom of Poseidon, where he died.

"Why didn't Apollo smite me instead of Icarus?" Daedalus recalled thinking then. "I was much more guilty of transgressing in his realm."

Consumed by grief, Daedalus after losing Icarus glided to a landfall on an island nearer to the Anatolian coast than to the Peloponnese. He had been on that isle only a short while when the great tsunami birthed by the earthquake at Crete cast upon those far shores the lifeless body of his son. Daedalus buried Icarus there and afterwards took up residence on the island. "I reasoned that I was still alive because Apollo wanted me to experience—to suffer—the loss of my son, and to find a way to atone for ignoring him, the true sun god."

Seeking a way to do so, Daedalus then moved many times, from island to island, steadily west, until at last he reached Sicily's southern coast, where lemons grew large as grapefruits and fields bowed beneath the weight of their grain. Daedalus accepted earthly patronage from Cocalus, the ruler there—materials, workshops, and apprentices, in the expectation that he would thereafter work for the glory of Apollo. Daedalus did, building temples, grottoes, monuments, and for Cocalus a hillside palace so ingeniously constructed that it could be defended by a handful of stalwarts. Years flew by without lessening the pain of Daedalus's permanently broken heart.

Information reached him that Minos had survived the collapse of the Cretan palace and empire, and that the old king, upon learning of the architectural and sculptural marvels then rising on the southern coast of Sicily, had deduced the likely identity of their fabricator, Daedalus.

Shortly thereafter, a small fleet of armed warships appeared in the waters off Agrigento near the castle that Daedalus had constructed for Cocalus.

Off the lead boat stepped a grizzled man who announced that he was on a pilgrimage to the Apollonian temple and to Cocalus's palace, looking for the answer to an enigmatic riddle. The disguised pilgrim was Minos and the riddle was what he bore in his hand, a chambered nautilus shell; he offered a prize for figuring a way through the shell's intricate maze.

While Minos was resting in a suite reserved for A-list visitors, Cocalus passed the nautilus to Daedalus. The artificer was unable to ignore the challenge of this puzzle, and arrogant enough to believe he could solve it. Arrogance! It is the prerogative and the vulnerability of artists no less than of potentates, don't you agree? I know, I know—you've had a touch of it yourselves, now and then. For some of us, more than a touch. Even when telling me this story, Daedalus could not resist boasting of his ingenuity.

"To solve the puzzle was simplicity itself, Asterion. I dabbed a bit of honey on one side of the shell, and into the other introduced a hungry ant to which I'd attached a tiny thread."

"Scarlet, of course?"

"Yes. The ant, as I knew it would, sensed its way through the coils to the honey. I then removed the creature but left the thread in place."

When Cocalus handed the completed puzzle to Minos, the latter insisted that only one man could have solved this conundrum, and then demanded that Cocalus return his escaped slave, Daedalus.

To Cocalus a brother king's appeal for the primacy of property rights had some appeal, and was reinforced by the large foreign fleet that Cocalus could see in the harbor. On the other horn, Daedalus had proved himself quite useful in Agrigento, and might be even more so in the future. So Cocalus made Minos an offer that the Cretan king could not politely refuse: Stay the night, have a warm bath, and share a feast with him and his three lovely daughters—virgins consecrated to the worship of Apollo—and in the morning, depart with Daedalus in tow.

Minos headed for the baths. Cocalus's daughters were so smitten with Apollo that they believed a murder performed to protect the sun god's chief artificer, Daedalus, would be a sin forgiven almost in advance of its commission. They plied Minos with wine and peek-a-boo veils and then placed more and more heated stones in the water. Soon Minos, who had himself set many a trap, was thoroughly poached.

And buried. At Agrigento Daedalus made a lovely tomb for his former patron, and resisted the impulse to decorate it with nautilus shells or labyrinths.

Yet after fashioning this tomb Daedalus constructed no further triumphs, preferring to rest the hands that had seldom been idle, and to bask in Apollo's warm rays until the time arrived for Hermes to escort him to the court of his next patron, Hades. That had since occurred. "Now the smelter is being smelted, Asterion. My spirit is being fused with the essence of Hephaestus, the smith among the gods. We will soon take the new name of Vulcan."

The process of amalgamation involved repeated baths in the Phlegethon to leach away Daedalus's remaining human aspects. This process, Daedalus informed me, was just like the lost-wax process in which a jewel was sculpted in wax, then surrounded by a mold of sand and plaster into which liquid metal was next poured; the wax melted and ran out a bottom hole, leaving behind in the mold the metallic version of the sculpture. "My power is growing, Asterion, even as my body dissolves; I can now speak to the essence of metals; Sulphur, for instance, is rather sweet once you get to know her."

Not long after Daedalus vanished into the Phlegethon I saw across the Acheron the shade of Minos. Knowing now how he had died, I had not expected to encounter him looking so vibrant. Had he not been subjected in Netherworld to the gauntlet formed by the many he had grievously hurt? That would've been quite a party. I'd not been invited to it. That disturbed me even though I had mostly given up my anger—one of the glories of Hades' domain is to no longer be troubled by anger, envy, jealousy and other pesky human emotions. We need not be bothered by these now, based, as they were, in the former twin threats of death and the swiftness with which time passes, both of these being irrelevant to us now.

"You are surprised that I appear so well, my Minotaur," Minos said. "I shall tell you about it, because, you know, we are actually cousins, and because you were always my favorite—the best part of me, the purest, the closest to my essential spirit."

"Your fondness for me was expressed in odd ways. And I reject the idea that I was the best part of you—the worst, perhaps."

"You knew what you had to do in the labyrinth, and you did it very well and with admirable abandon, Asterion. You executed and frightened and terrorized—"

"You forced me to do those tasks so you would not sully your hands."

"I had little choice, Asterion; the ruler of an empire is beset by continual demands."

"Nonsense. For what you did to the world you should be in fetters for eternity."

Minos chuckled, a sound seldom heard in Netherworld. "I see that you have formed as distinctly wrong an impression of this realm as you had of the one above. You have become a convert to the Great Negative Confession."

"What?"

"An old-fashioned Egyptian notion, Asterion. It celebrates the common man, who, when he is about to cross through the gate into the Underworld, can honestly recite a long list of large sins that he has *not* committed: 'I have not flooded my neighbor's fields, I have not caused vast numbers of people to die in war, I have not enslaved whole populaces,' and so on. That is because the common man's sins are ... common. And small. Petty theft, trifling infidelities, a murder or two at the most—picayune matters that should not prevent him from sailing through the final judgment and earning a happy afterlife. The common man loves that Negative Confession because he knows who it is that cannot truthfully recite it—the powerful men among men, the kings and the generals and the religious chiefs. Accordingly, the common man supposes that in the afterlife the big shots will suffer in due proportion to the power they once wielded; and that their suffering will be a satisfaction to the now-dead common man and his colleagues, recompense for the miserable existences they led when in the Middle Realm. Wrong!

"How foolish of the common man, Asterion, to presume that the same standards apply to the powerful as to him." Minos shook his head. That head, and indeed his entire person, had grown more massive and imposing even as we talked. "Why, Asterion, why after all that you have personally been through, do you still cling to such a naive concept?"

"I believe in justice."

"No you don't; you believe in the vengeance of the powerless," Minos said. "That's petty vengeance, Asterion, and let me tell you, the gods laugh at it and so do the powerful, above and below. How often do you think it is, in the Middle Realm, that the powerful are really brought low, are commensurately punished? You know it's never been very often, and now—well, let's face it: the heyday of the Egyptian pharaonic dynasties is gone. And with that has vanished the moment in the sun of all those who believed in posthumous retribution on the previously powerful as a balance to their mortal lives of misery. Do you think that Zeus, Poseidon, and Hades give a hoot about such balance? Of course they don't. What they care about are such ideas as progress. Order. Efficiency.

"Take Order, for instance: do you think Order is easy to produce? In the Middle Realm? It was difficult enough for me to impose what I thought of as stability and harmony, and then when I wasn't expecting it everything collapsed. The gods had dictated that my empire was to be disrupted because it was in the way to creating a new order in the world. Do you think that was a piece of cake for me? Oh, I tell you, Asterion, when Crete's cities were destroyed, when my fleet drowned at anchor, when I had to watch Theseus escape with Ariadne and Phaedra, and Daedalus and Icarus fly away, I was brought very low.

"Eventually, though, the gods helped me to understand that the loss of my empire had been no more than unfortunate collateral damage," Minos continued. "Their need was to make way for creating a new empire, a PanHellenic one, firmly rooted in the worship of the male trinity of Zeus, Poseidon, and Hades—a task for which the Peloponnese mainland is a far better base than Crete. I could understand the gods' need to shift to having earthly power wielded by men from the mainland who were better able to conquer new horizons. My job as the earthly Minos was done. With your help, while alive I had wrenched power from that retrograde domain of women who had no vision other than the perpetuating of the race, clearing the way for the future. Deny, if you can, that that job had been done well."

I was silent.

"After my initial scourging here—just a light scorch—Zeus, Hades, and Poseidon restored me to power. More: Uncle Hades gave me a new task, a reorganization of Netherworld that had awaited my arrival to be implemented."

Minos now turned aside, and I glanced in the direction he faced, at two other approaching shades, each as imposing as Minos had become, twice as massive as any human shade, full-bearded and impressively ancient, and all three exuding auras of menace and finality. Behind them the halvoids were erecting a raised platform for them. Minos greeted the more fair-haired ancient first, and I understood this to be Rhadamanthys, his blood brother, summoned from the Isles of the Blest. The other magisterial shade, darker though more ancient in countenance, was Aeacus, another son of Zeus, who when alive had been a harsh and obdurate king. Indicative of Aeacus's attitude toward humans was the name he had applied to his subjects in the middle realm: Myrmidons, the ant-people.

Yes, my fellow shades: That was the beginning of the three-judge panel, a brilliant move to free top management from the workaday, onerous task of adjudicating the former lives of newly-arrived shades and of allotting to each their burden of punishment. Now neither Hades nor his wife has to dirty their metaphysical hands! When the recently dead alight from Charon's ferry, they are assessed, not as they might have hoped, by the gods, but by the bureaucrats.

Of the three judicial presences, Rhadamanthys is the more benign, Aeacus the more inclined to infer evil in the supplicants, and Minos the most powerful because he is the swing vote. What a perfect choice for that position—a king who already knows that when it comes to judging human beings, fairness is not the deciding factor, and who has a good nose for the importance of humiliation.

Since the ascension of this truculent trio, many formerly powerful humans have regularly had their sins excused for no other reason than their Minos-like claim that their actions had moved the Middle Realm forward. Take Attila the Hun, for example—you don't see him here, do you? Or Hitler? Stalin? Mao? Idi Amin? No. They've gone back to the Middle Realm, even though the evil in them was not nearly well enough expunged, and even though they murdered on a scale that made us serial killers appear as real pikers. Three million dead here, six million dead there, forty million in China, yet the spirits of the mass annihilators are not held in Netherworld in perpetuity. Rather, they've graduated, returned to the Middle Realm despite what I believe to have been their incomplete metamorphoses.

148

I count the mass killers' restoration to the Middle Realm as a failing of the gods. They disagree. They assert that my accusation is due to my absence of true understanding, is a failing of my human side—that I, no less than full humans, have a characteristic blind spot, an assumption that evil is capable of being permanently vanquished. Evil is a shape-shifter, they say, and cannot ever be completely purged.

Speaking of human failings, I was interested to chat with my sisters Ariadne and Phaedra, when they arrived, separately, at the near bank of the Styx; but I had hardly begun to hear Ariadne's tale when the entire hierarchy of Hades' Hacienda flew into an uproar, and had to deal with a pair of passengers in Charon's ferry whose arrival brought the whole Netherworld operation to a standstill: two living men, Theseus and Pirithous.

"That son-of-a-bitch!" Phaedra blurted out.

"Which one?" I asked.

"Could be either," Ariadne laughed. "But I think she's referring to Theseus. After all, he married both of us, in turn."

At the arrival of Theseus and Pirithous, Charon's ferry sprung a leak, Cerberus's three heads barked uncontrollably in a three-part cacophony that Bach might have envied, and Minos and his fellow judges became apoplectic, for these visitors seemed not to be subject to the demigods' imprecations or their juridical dicta. The two humans debarked from the ferry and made their way along the darkling plain, seeking something. Quite apart from the mystery of how two living men had been transported to Hades' domain, the presence of the heroes occasioned consternation in other ways. Although the pair's swords and arrows made no indentations in the amorphous halvoids that surrounded them, neither could the halvoid extensions of Hades' will restrain the humans' living flesh. Steadily the pair moved into the continental desert. Soon the suicides on the barren hills stopped flaying their neighbors, and the knots that had tied the spirits of the adulterers to unobtainable phantoms began to unravel.

Most alarming to me was that Ariadne and Phaedra forsook the calm grove between cypress and poplar, where we had been standing, to follow Theseus. Evidently both were still attracted to their ex-husband. When these two female shades tugged at Theseus he seemed to react, to feel a slight sensation, and he responded by looking around, although he could not actually see them.

"He's come for me," Phaedra insisted.

"No. For me, his first love," Ariadne countered.

I was curious about this man who had slain me—after all, until this moment I had only seen him in drag.

His physique and visage reminded me of Androgeos: The chiseled profile worthy of a statue, the supple limbs, the only moderately high forehead, a man whose rightful post was at the helm of a ship, looking for danger to face, cities and beautiful women to conquer, and enemies to slay. What he and Pirithous were searching for we did not know, and so could neither help them nor deter them. Phaedra confided that Pirithous was a notorious carouser, a king of Thessaly who would always rather roam than rule. He and Theseus had together fought a great battle with the centaurs, and from then on had been drinking buddies.

Their footsteps in Hades' domain began a startling geologic upheaval. The fires on the desert plain, and the sinuous stream of Lethe, crept closer to the living wanderers, as though Hades was positioning these features of the landscape in their path. The sulfurous mists then parted to reveal, in the distance, an inviting mountain. The visitors headed in that direction. The rest of us who were able to follow did so, up a hill and onto a slope that led gently down to a riverbank. The river was cool and lovely, as few other things in this domain were. Across from it fires blazed and their smoke beclouded the desert, although the mountain beyond remained visible. The riverbank seemed an ideal spot at which to pause before tackling the fiery zone that stood athwart the path leading to the mountain. The rocks at the river's edge invited a short rest.

My labyrinth-honed instincts told me this was a trap, but I could do nothing about it, nor did I want to. The mortals walked right into it, sitting down on the cool stone embankment, dipping their hands into the liquid and lifting them to their lips. They drank, and instanter ceased to move.

The new river then dried up and disappeared, the smoky plain and lofty mountain vanished, and what remained in the grove were two mostly immobile statues. These now faced two thrones, each topped by flaring flames. I knew these latter to be the seats of Hades and of Persephone, the goddess who spent only part of each year in the Underworld.

"Now, at least, we can examine these interlopers," boomed Hades-the-flame, enlarging to the size of a healthy torch.

His companion flame emitted a tinkling, soprano laugh, and flickered about the heroes, who breathed although they were otherwise immobile. "Pirithous," sighed the female flame.

"You know this mortal?" demanded Hades.

"He pledged to rescue me from your kingdom," Persephone responded.

"How romantic. I've allowed you to have your fun when you're out of my realm, Persephone, but for him to pursue you to Netherworld is insufferable. Perhaps I should wipe his mind clean and then send him back to the Middle Realm, so he would not know you above."

Persephone fretted.

We watched her—'we' meaning myself, Ariadne, Phaedra, Minos, Rhadamanthys, Aeacus, Pasiphaë, Vulcan, the Furies, and assorted others who had convened in the grove of Hades around the near-statues Theseus and Pirithous. Never before and never since has there been such a convention of the dead, the semi-dead, the godly, the ungodly, the heroic, the villainous, the semi-divine, and the semi-bovine.

Raucous cries were heard: Some of the more anonymous shades called for condemning the interlopers to Tartarus's care, others called for returning them empty-handed back to the Middle Realm. Some were for punishing Persephone, some were

151

for exalting her right to choose her lovers. Ariadne and Phaedra loudly refused to relinquish their right to harrow Theseus, even though they still felt lust for him. Vulcan declared himself prepared to foreswear his vengeance on Theseus, which dated back five generations, to the time when Theseus's ancestors had wrested the throne of Athens from Daedalus's own ancestors.

Alarums came from several further quarters of the landscape. The ground rumbled. Rivers overflowed their banks. Clouds of black smoke swirled about in a menacing way. Hades' flame nearly snuffed out.

"A decision must soon be reached on this matter of Theseus and Pirithous," Hades boomed to the three judges, bucking the matter down to the bureaucracy. "The appearance of the living in the kingdom of the dead has attracted the attention of my brother, Poseidon."

This was cause for alarm because, as we watchers all knew, the universe exists in a delicate balance of power among the three brother gods. Should the necessary separation of Hades' Netherworld from the Middle Realm not hold, there could be unleashed the War of the Kingdoms, earth versus sky, sea versus the depths, and depths versus earth, which could lead to the ultimate doomsday, the emasculation of all three gods, Zeus, Poseidon and Hades, and the return of Chaos, the original maker of worlds.

Just then the never-solid ground beneath us began to crack and split, and from its fissures arose an enormous, many-tentacled yet handsome sea-creature, larger and more terrifying than any being on Hades' plain. Liquids oozed from its every limb, swamping the nearby shades.

"Poseidon!" the torch said.

"It is I," the sea-creature answered, the voice not so much coming from a mouth as from its entire corpus. "Why have you not condemned these mortals? Instruct your judges to kill and punish, Hades!"

"Your roar will not intimidate my judges in this realm, brother."

152

"Then direct them to decide, forthwith. I remove my protection from Theseus, so that he can die."

Minos, Rhadamanthus, and Aeacus appeared uncomfortable at the thought of having to choose between the wishes of Hades and those of Poseidon. Yet all three judges, as sons of Zeus, enjoyed some immunity from the power of Poseidon and Hades, and this translated into a modified degree of judicial autonomy.

"Let the trial begin," Hades insisted.

"Poseidon, who has ever favored Theseus in life, shall speak against him here," Minos said from the bench, preparing to begin the proceedings. "Who shall speak for Theseus?"

The entire assemblage seemed struck dumb at the thought. In the presence of such mighty beings, who could dare be anything but mute?

"Asterion speaks for Theseus," I piped up. "And the defense wishes to call a few witnesses."

"Phaedra, my sister: You committed suicide to get away from Theseus, yet you say he should be sent back to the Middle Realm unharmed?"

"I do. My tale begins with your death, Asterion, and with the escape of Daedalus and Icarus. The entire palace of Knossos was crumbling beneath me—the stairways, the balconies, the candelabra, everything was falling. I was sure I'd be killed. Ariadne and Theseus found me. Then, with what was left of Theseus's group of fourteen we ran out of the palace. We only lost a few Athenian comrades before reaching the harbor. It was the first time Theseus saved my life."

"How did you survive the great wave?"

"The sailors didn't want to haul up the anchor, because as the tremors became larger all the other ships were clinging to their anchorage. So Theseus cut that rope. When the big wave hit, all the ships that still had anchors were drowned, while our untethered ship flowed with the waters far out into the open sea. What a celebration we had then, Asterion—lots of drinking of toasts and congratulating each other for being very smart and very brave. Theseus and Ariadne were married on board by a sailor who was also a priest. I was the bridesmaid: Just fourteen—can you imagine?—and not a very good drinker. I became seasick, and then fell asleep. Next thing I knew, it was morning and we were entering the harbor at Naxos to buy a replacement anchor. What a bad choice of place to do that!"

"Stick to the facts, Phiddy," Minos roared.

"Oh, Daddy, what's a fact anyway?"

"Please continue to tell us about Theseus, Queen Phaedra," I jumped in.

"On Naxos, while Theseus and his crew scoured the port to find a new anchor, Ariadne went for a walk in the hills, where she was captured by the god Dionysos, who took her away forever."

"Took her away?"

"To be his bride, yes," Phaedra nodded.

"Didn't Theseus object?"

"What could he do, Asterion? Theseus said it was the will of the god. Why do you laugh, Asterion? It was a terrible and sad thing to have happen."

"Ariadne betrayed her father Minos, betrayed her lover Daedalus, betrayed her most fervent admirer—me—and then, after a single night, betrayed her rescuing prince and husband, Theseus!"

"Theseus was very upset, Asterion. He cried for days on the journey home. He was so distraught that he even made an awful mistake."

Phaedra went on to tell how Theseus, morose at having lost his wife to a god, forgot to change the ship's sails from black to white, the signal he had earlier agreed with his father Aegeus to display were the Athenians able to bring down Minos's empire and escape. King Aegeus, on a promontory at Piraeus, spotted the black sails far in the distance, assumed from that signal that his son had died, and threw himself into the sea. Thus did

Prince Theseus come home not to the strains of a victory march but to the dirge of mourning.

"And was soon crowned king?" I asked.

"Yes."

"Then the black sails were no mistake, Phaedra, but a way to urge Aegeus to commit suicide so that Theseus could have the throne without waiting for his father to die of old age."

"Theseus is not a devious thinker, Asterion. He's straightforward and blunt."

"Theseus crushed your father's empire, killed your furry brother Asterion, abandoned your dear sister Ariadne, and 'accidentally' caused his own father to leap into the sea—and you still think he's terrific?"

"Back then he was certainly my hero, the greatest man I'd ever seen."

"And so you married him."

"Not just then, no. First I married Deucalion, and we had three children, and his business prospered and I insisted that we move back to Crete, where the schools were better. Then the business went bust and he was lost at sea."

"That took how long?"

"Fourteen years."

"And then you married Theseus?"

"Yes. I mean, for him, after Antiope, who was quite the Amazon—they'd fought side by side, you know—he wanted someone a little less, uh, volcanic, and I, well, Deucalion had been nice and all, but kind of bland ... and ..."

"Phiddy!"

"All right, Daddy. If you must know, Theseus was the complete opposite of you. You gave up marauding for ruling, and he, well, once the honeymoon was over—you know the type: 'I came, I saw, I conquered, I abandoned.' Out carousing with Pirithous. If they weren't battling centaurs, they were partying with them. A little war here, a little adultery there ..."

"But you were still married to him when you died, weren't you?"

"Yes, well, that's not the point I—"

155

"We will decide relevance, Phaedra," Minos said. "Your witness, Poseidon."

I was not through with Phaedra but had no possibility of objecting. From this court there was no appeal.

"You betrayed Theseus, did you not?" Poseidon, in accusatory mode.

"I tried to. With his son from his previous marriage, Hippolytus. Just fifteen. We met during a retreat for the Eleusinian mysteries."

"Both chasing happiness, no doubt?"

"He reminded me forcefully of Icarus at the age when I had loved him. Blonde, fair of face, beautifully muscled. I built Hippolytus a theater. He paid me no attention. I gave him a wondrous bow for the hunt. Didn't bring me so much as a dove. I pursued him to Troezen, where he was studying, and made him an offer: We would unite, I would teach him about love, and together we would push Theseus off his throne."

"Nonetheless, he rejected you."

"Yes. Probably only liked men, anyway. Worse: He said he'd tattle on his wicked stepmother to his father, once Theseus returned home."

"So you hung yourself."

"And blamed the boy in a note, yes."

"A note that caused Theseus to call upon me to kill the boy, which I obligingly did—another death for which you are responsible."

"And for which I have been punished in Tartarus. But I never blamed Theseus, although I had cause, and you shouldn't blame him for coming here."

"And why not?"

"For the same reason as I don't: Because he was and is just being … male."

"Did Dionysos make you an offer you couldn't refuse?" I asked my next witness, Ariadne.

"Absolutely," she said, and told the tale. While Theseus was searching for an anchor, she led some of the mature women toward the peak of Mount Drios. They were half-way up its grassy slopes when they encountered a long-haired, well-muscled, and nearly undraped young man who carried in one hand a fennel-staff with ivy bunched at the tip, and in the other a jar of newly-pressed wine. This charming young man offered the thirsty women a drink from his jar, and when they all had had their fill and discovered that the jar would not empty, they understood themselves to be in the presence of a god, who named himself to them as Dionysos, and revealed his cloven hoofs. When he used his wand to stimulate them all to orgasm, their reverence for him increased. The god then proposed that Ariadne and her friends become his celebrants and priestesses. Their obeisance would be light, and they would spend their days and nights roaming the island, dancing, singing, drinking wine, and fornicating to their hearts' delight. He would provide them with food and would relieve them of cares. Their duties would be to occasionally water the vines and the ivy and those pine trees that had drooping cones, and to lead the islanders in revels at various times each year. They needn't bother tending the more usual crops, and there would be none of that ponderous, furrow-browed, fertility business associated with the Goddess of No Name. Dionysos was the god of revels, not of responsibility.

"By accepting Dionysos' offer, I could be as unfettered as I had hoped to be upon escaping the palace and labyrinth. To live with Theseus would merely have been to substitute a jailer husband for a jailer father. To worship Dionysos was to be free to enjoy life."

"But there were conditions."

"When we ran out of other food, he would send us a sheep, a cow, or a covey of doves and we would have to engage in the holy rituals of sparagmos and omophagia."

"Please explain."

"Sparagmos, the tearing apart of a living animal. Omophagia, the eating of raw flesh."

"What I did, in the labyrinth! And you preferred that half-goat, Dionysos, to the half-bull, me?"

"Sparagmos and omophagia are as much a part of the Dionysian way as the ceaseless drinking and fornication. Savagery and revelry are not opposites but facets of a single practice."

"And how came you to Hades' Domain?"

My sister became more thoughtful. "At sunrise one day, when I was completely drunk and had spent the night dancing, I felt as though my body was an encumbrance that I no longer required. My spirit was floating, trying to achieve union with the early morning mists on Mount Drios. My sisters in the band were hungry, so I permitted them to kill me and eat my raw flesh, and did not begrudge them the sustenance. Next thing I knew, I was in Charon's ferry."

"My congratulations: That is the death I imagined for myself but never attained. Your witness, sire."

"Ariadne, did you seek permission from Dionysos to die in that manner?"

"No," Ariadne admitted to Poseidon.

"So you betrayed Dionysos as you had earlier betrayed your true goddess, as well as your mother, your father, your brother Asterion, and your husband?"

"I merely did what I wanted to do, rather than what they wanted me to do."

"And Theseus has done the same?"

"Exactly, yes. And that is why you seek to kill him now."

"That's enough out of you, Arie," Minos cut in. "Take her away—take both of these women to the harrowing ground."

"A moment, Great Judge," I said. "Let them stay for the summations and the verdict."

Poseidon magnified in size, and his stentorian roar cowed all who came within its reach. Pointing his multitude of arms at the rapidly solidifying bodies of Theseus and Pirithous, he said: "Theseus is a destroyer in the guise of a rescuing hero. Pirithous is a killer in the guise of a lover. By forcing their way into Netherworld, these mortals have offended all the gods and upset the order of the universe. They aim to upend it even further by stealing Queen Persephone, despite her husband, my brother, Hades, ordering her to remain in the Netherworld. Theseus and Pirithous wish to defy the working-out of destinies, which are only for the gods to set. They are guilty of the primary sin of mortals, arrogating to themselves the power of the gods. Only by condemning them perpetually to the care of Tartarus can the rule of the gods remain unchallenged."

Shouts of assent rose from the shades on the Hadean plain, from the billions of former mortals who had not themselves been able to escape death. The panel of judges appeared ready to accede to Poseidon's reasoning. Minos now gave me leave to speak.

"Theseus is the man who killed me, my lords, yet I defend him. I do so because what he has come here to do is necessary. He must return Persephone to the Middle Realm. Now I do admit that his thinking ... is a bit thin. He believes that by returning her to the Middle Realm he will restore order there and release the world from the grip of winter, during which no crops grow. But that is not what he will do by returning her above. What he will do is restore anarchy and uncertainty to the realm of human beings. And that, my lords, he *must* do!"

The shades tried to shout me down, but my voice strengthened.

"More, my lords: You must permit Theseus to complete his mission! For if Theseus and Pirithous are kept here, along with Persephone, there will be no uncertainty left in the Middle Realm, and Persephone's permanent presence below will in itself bring about the end of the Middle Realm."

More roars of disapproval.

"There is no renewal without death, my lords. Before completing my argument, I demand that the goddess Persephone show herself in her true form."

The rivers of Netherworld crested and frothed, the desert sands shifted, hills formed and reformed, and the noxious smoke came suffocatingly near.

159

"You know not what you ask, Minotaur," Poseidon warned.

"I am aware of the dangers of seeing the true form of a god," I declared loudly, "but that is essential to the solution of the problems facing us."

Hades-the-flame cracked and crinkled. A moment later, the flame on the adjoining throne disappeared, replaced—indeed, overwhelmed—by a huge and ancient female figure, smelly, hairy-visaged, with pendulous breasts and swollen abdomen.

Everyone gasped.

I smiled. She was she whom I had envisioned as the Goddess of No Name. She, the fecund. She, the mother of us all. She, the maker of inner and outer labyrinths. There could be no other explanation for Persephone's dilatory nature.

"The harshness and fickleness of the goddess of the changeable seasons troubles the world, my lords—but these very qualities are essential to the health of the Middle Realm. And that is why I beseech you: Let her return there, annually. But not in her present form. It is too harsh for the world, now. Soften her frightening aspects by including within her the spirits of my sisters, Ariadne and Phaedra. My dark-haired Ariadne, trained by Dionysos, shall provide the ever-youthful facet of Persephone, the one that awakens life in the spring; and my fair-haired Phaedra, full of experience and unfulfilled longings, shall be the golden, mature ripening of the fall harvest."

The roar subsided somewhat, so I careened on.

"I request that Theseus be returned to the Middle Realm to continue his conquests and his world-shaking. Pirithous is another matter. I propose that he remain in Hades' domain, condemned as much for the sin of attempting to own the goddess Persephone as for having fomented this trip to Netherworld and thereby bringing the universe to the brink of chaos. Were these dispositions to be granted, our crisis would be settled."

There was a moment of silence.

Then Poseidon quietly said, "I have taught you very well, my Minotaur."

The judges conferred among themselves; but before they

could announce a decision, a thunderbolt imploded in our midst. When the dust cleared, there stood before us the greatest of all heroes, Heracles, he who was both alive and beyond life. In his infancy Heracles had sucked a few drops of milk from the breast of Hera, the wife of Zeus, and had become, at least in part, immortal.

"A message from the elder brother," Poseidon chortled.

Heracles, Zeus's creature, picked up a recuperating Theseus, and with him ascended out of Netherworld—in effect, carrying out the panel's decision before they could do so. Pirithous, as I had recommended, remained behind in Hades' house, turned to stone, a status of warning, perpetually perched on the precipice of Lethe. And then it was time for the goddess Persephone, having assimilated the shades of Ariadne and Phaedra, to return above, in full knowledge that she could not stay in the Middle Realm indefinitely and would return to Hades' side, winter after winter.

If my terrific rhetoric could get Theseus out, and Persephone too, why couldn't it get me out? I'm sure you were wondering that. And I did want to go, you know. None of us is content to stay below, no matter what awfulness might lurk ahead for us in our next lives.

That subject I discussed with Poseidon, near the grove of Lethe and Mnemosyne. The form in which he had shown himself to us, a multi-tentacled sea-creature, was in the process of dissolving into a whirlpool of viscous saline.

"Have I not been punished enough for my sins, great lord and father?"

"Yes, Asterion."

"Then why must I remain in Hades' House?"

"Because your crimes must be forgotten in the Middle Realm. Their example is a continuing danger to the gods."

"Then why have the gods stolen my essence and granted it to Dionysos?"

161

"We need to make ourselves and our offspring more palatable to mortals, or we'll vanish. Dionysos's form appears to be more life-giving and therefore more acceptable to humans than a death-dealing minotaur."

"More life-giving? Dionysos who insists on sparagmos and omophagia, killing and eating the flesh of sacrificial animals while they're still alive?"

"Humans will soon forget about the violent parts of the Dionysian ritual and will celebrate that god as the symbol of carefree revels, as a harmless diversionary. His festivals will have no more relation to the harsh realities of the Middle Realm than do the games in which men with swords kill horned bulls have to do with your murderous struggle with Theseus in the labyrinth."

"Then why not release me?"

"The Middle Realm no longer has use for a minotaur. Nor, for that matter, for a snake-headed Medusa, nor for a half-horse centaur. If we old gods are too magnificent and terrifying for humans to contemplate, then our offspring are also too awful, so we must all stay out of human consciousness. The tenor of the Middle Realm is shifting, Asterion. As its leadership moves from the Minoan Seas to the Mediterranean, its people become less reflexively barbaric. They are rapidly losing their desire to be constantly reminded of the horrific nature of the gods. Mortals now want gods they can love and that will love them back, not gods whom they have to fear all the time. They want kinder, gentler gods, not those who seem to constantly seek bloody vengeance."

"If there is no Minotaur above, sire, then humankind will create their own omnivorous killers. And those will kill not only for their rulers, but to satisfy their own terrible dreams."

"A small price for humankind to pay, Asterion, in exchange for being permitted to live in a world without daily vengeful gods."

"This longing for benevolence without balancing horror, sire, is so juvenile."

"It is human."

"Yes, but is it necessary?"

"If we gods do not make ourselves and our creatures palatable to mortals, then we risk oblivion. And that, we cannot permit."

"I cannot imagine that humankind will never have less need to fear Hades' domain, sire, or even your own."

"All of us fierce spirits are having to learn that we must bend to humanity's inexorable evolution. You, Asterion, you were the vanguard of change. At a time when regular mortals still did not understand that the domain of the Goddess of No Name and her priestesses was a labyrinth from which there was no escape and no progress, you showed them that. Your magisterial murdering compromised the labyrinth, and your own distinguished demise brought down the entire structure and the empire for which the labyrinth had served as center. You have enabled mortals to now move beyond the labyrinth and into the next stage of human development."

"Which is?"

"A stage in which restless males, such as your executioner, Theseus, as they conquer the world will spread civilization from one place to the next and the next and the next, creating cities from deserts, homes and farms from forests, and knowledge from ignorance. Your sensing of Theseus's role in that future is why you defended him here on the Judgment Plain, is it not?"

"His audacity gave me hope."

"The Middle Realm needs a Theseus, Asterion. But it no longer has need of a lone Minotaur. And that is your triumph: Because you so thoroughly inhabited minotaurdom, so well expressed human compassion along with the animal urge to survive at any cost, you have saved the world from the need to have a future minotaur—and for that matter, from having to be vexed by any half-animal, mixed-beast monster. Tomorrow's villains, and the horror they promulgate, will only be mortals."

"Then let me disappear."

"You will be forgotten, but you won't vanish completely."

"I won't?"

"You cannot. Henceforth every man and woman will harbor a minotaur within. They will know, as you now know, that they have the capacity to destroy the world around them. And they will hope, as you still hope, that they and their brothers and sisters have the strength to control that urge to destroy."

My fellow residents of this pleasant grove between the cypress and the poplar, you who have heard my story to its end, you will shortly return to the Middle Realm. I wish you the speed of dreams, and the fabulous luxury of forgetting your pasts and beginning anew. I will remain here, as I have for fifty centuries and as I shall do until the end of the universe. My plea—and it is only a plea—is that you bear, deep within you, the knowledge of my truth: Have courage and do not fear death—or life. In your next incarnation, each of you must resolve to make yourself the sovereign of your own labyrinth of joy and pain, and to set as your task the recognition of and empathy with the labyrinths of others.

As billions of people do so, humanity's labyrinths will combine and multiply in space and in time. Every door will be an entry and an exit, a dead end and a revelation. Every puzzle will have a solution, and every solution will itself be a puzzle. Humanity will have immense knowledge and yet not exhaust the essence of things. I, the Minotaur, know all and I know very little; I lived but did not live; I died but I cannot die. I imagine a realm to which you shall return but that I shall never again visit, a realm of verdant fields and azure oceans and flawless skies. A cloud wafts on breezes until it settles comfortably from nothingness into something, becoming an island lapped by the immense, primordial waters. On that island, bathed in sunlight, creatures stir and wonder and clash, and call upon unseen powers in voices urgent and compelling. "Answer our prayers," they implore the gods. "Tell us why we live and why we must die. Tell us why we are male and female. Tell us why ecstasy and terror exist and cannot be separated. Tell us why we can never be satisfied. Tell us why you made us in your image."

In Netherworld the great god Hades quivers with antici-pation. In the sky the great god Zeus senses the excitement of impending action. In an abyss in the vastness of oceanic Middle Realm the great god Poseidon laughs a fecund laugh. The bub-ble of his laughter ascends toward the surface, growing brighter and more corporeal as it rises. Soon, very soon, five thousand years from now and five thousand years ago and in the very next moment, Poseidon's answer to the recurring, impudent ques-tions of the human race will take the shape of a pure white bull on the white sands of the beach at Crete.

About the Author

Tom Shachtman holds a B.S. in animal behavior, an M.F.A. in playwriting, and has a body of published and produced work that includes eighteen non-fiction books, such as *The Day America Crashed*, *Rumspringa: To Be or Not To Be Amish*, and the latest, *The Founding Fortunes*; short novels, including *Beachmaster* and *The Eagle's Claw*; books for children, such as *Growing Up Masai*; and documentaries for ABC, CBS, NBC, and PBS, the most recent being *Absolute Zero and the Conquest of Cold*, a two-hour *Nova* based on his book of the same name. He has also collaborated on a dozen books, among them *Whoever Fights Monsters* (with Robert K. Ressler), considered the definitive study of serial killers.

Q & A with Tom Shachtman
Regarding
The Memoir of the Minotaur

Q: Whence came this crazy idea?

A: As a college senior, while taking three courses in three different departments I had to read Greek tragedy in each, and overdosed. I was then also completing a degree in experimental psychology, investigating (and learning to appreciate) intelligence in animals. Since I didn't like torturing lab rats in mazes, and had had some early success in writing for the theater, I went on to graduate school and an MFA in drama, but retained from my lab days enough understanding of animal minds to depict a character whose half-bull side will not be ignored! Which also reminds me to mention, as precursors to *Memoir of the Minotaur*, some writing that also benefits from my studies of animal behavior, my trilogy of short novels, *Beachmaster*, *Wavebender*, and *Driftwhistler*, whose protagonist is a California sea lion, a self-taught sculptor of natural materials. As you undoubtedly know, James Joyce wrote *Portrait of the Artist as a Young Man*, which Dylan Thomas mocked in writing *Portrait of the Artist as a Young Dog*, so I felt no compunction about penning a "Portrait of the

Artist as a Young Sea-dog." From there it was just the flap of a flipper to a half-man-half-bull ...

I should also mention as influential Conrad Aiken's long poem "The Coming Forth by Day of Osiris Jones." In it, Aiken fuses the *Egyptian Book of the Dead* with the comic techniques of Harold Lloyd and Charlie Chaplin films, and with material from his father's medical notebooks. With Aiken's permission, I adapted the poem for an off-off-Broadway play, and it adopted me.

Q: Aren't you mainly a serious historian, with, egads, eighteen books on various eras, including three on the Revolutionary War?

A: Yes, and I love doing those; but inside of every serious non-fiction writer that I know, including me, there exists a raving comedic sensibility. At times that inside lunatic escapes, and when that happens, well, readers need to be very wary.

Second answer to same question: Writing history has forced me to become a better researcher. *Memoir of the Minotaur* benefits from my having visited catacombs and underground ossuaries in Europe, reading alternative mythologies, histories of volcanoes, numerical calculations, and even dictionaries, in which one can find forgotten yet extremely accurate words like "orchidate."

Q: Speaking of research, your Minotaur is a serial killer. A little bird told me that you co-wrote "the" book on serial killers.

A: Guilty! The late Robert K. Ressler, a former FBI guy and the virtual founder of the Behavioral Sciences Unit at Quantico, my co-author on *Whoever Fights Monsters* (1991), coined the term serial killer, interviewed lots of them, knew more about that subject than anyone else on earth—and imparted some of what he'd learned to me in the course of our writing three books together.

Q: What about all the sex in your book? Do you have a dirty mind?

A: We all do. The sexy parts of the *Minotaur* are not intended as descriptives but as theater of the imagination for the reader.

Q: Any other literary influences on your work?

A: The critic George Steiner wrote a classic critique, *Tolstoy or Dostoyevsky*, making the case that there are two kinds of story-telling, the Tolstoyan "epic tradition" that begins with Homer and describes things from the outside in, and the more modern, Dostoevskyan "internal" story-telling that starts in the mind and moves outward. I try to do both, but must confess to having read (and re-read) everything of Tolstoy's that has been translated into English and, I am ashamed to report, having never been able to finish a Dostoevsky novel, not to mention never getting past page 7 of a Henry James short story.

Q: What helped you the most in writing the book?

A: Choosing to have the Minotaur communicate his story to recently arrived souls in Hades' Domain, which allows me to use all of the last 5,000 years of recorded history as his platform and his context for speech.

Q: What, ahem, implements do you use in writing?

A: I write fiction first in longhand, which my grade-school age grandchildren refer to as "cursive." Writing an initial draft in longhand slows me down and frees me from the Curse of the Cursor, with its horrific blinking needle.

Q: What do you want readers to take from the book?

A: Beyond enjoyment, an appreciation that the people of the far past had to cope with the same sort of problems, stresses, and joys as we do now; and a respect for the power of myth to convey some of those basic sensations and feelings in more than realistic terms; and the understanding that potential humor exists in almost every aspect of human endeavor.

Q: Do you have any sage advice for readers of your book?

A: Buy two copies, so you can give one to that special other person without feeling deprived.